ARES IS MINE

GODS AND MONSTERS

MILA YOUNG

Cover art by Cover Reveal Designs

ISBN: 978-1795633031

BOOKS BY MILA YOUNG

HAVEN REALM SERIES
Hunted (Little Red Riding Hood Retelling)
Charmed (Arabian Nights Retelling)
Cursed (Beauty and the Beast Retelling)
Claimed (Little Mermaid Retelling)
Entangled (Rapunzel Retelling)
Dark Reflections (Snow White Retelling)

WICKED HEAT SERIES
Wicked Heat #1
Wicked Heat #2
Wicked Heat #3

SPIRIT SERIES
Spirit Of Christmas
Spirit Of Love

More on the way…

GODS AND MONSTERS

BY MILA YOUNG

Apollo Is Mine
Poseidon Is Mine
Ares Is Mine
Hades Is Mine

ARES IS MINE

"I'm not here to look for trouble," he said in a soft voice, as if he'd heard my thoughts. "You should know that by now."

I was starting to know Ares a little better, and he was nothing like what I'd first thought. Of course, I still remained wary of him, but that worry was born from stories I'd heard from others, and from what the history books said about him. I was realizing they were all wrong.

"Fine," I agreed. "But you're not dressed to train."

Ares pulled down his jeans.

"Jesus," I said when he stood in front of me with just his jock strap on, his package as clear as day. Were my cheeks burning up?

"Better?" He winked.

CHAPTER 1

Elyse

*M*agic and newfound energy filled me after my second death, and the power hummed under my skin like an adrenaline kick, as if I'd eaten a kilo of chocolate and washed it down with two gallons of energy drink. Getting out into the crisp air before the world woke up helped tame the power inside me. My life had changed so much since the gods arrived in town. Not to mention, Death, or X as we all called him, had been killing innocents and now was focusing his attention on me.

The sun crept over Chicago on Monday morning, turning the silvery quality of night into the brightest orange hues, and I powerwalked along an empty side-walk. My backpack sat over my shoulder with my camera, since this was the best time of day for photos. I worked as a freelance photographer because it was the easiest job I was good at, which I could maintain while I fought to save humans from whatever the gods sent our way. A nine-to-five just wouldn't cut it, and despite my struggles being divine in nature, I still had human bills to pay. The contrast staggered me sometimes.

I had a handful of recurring clients, mostly requiring photos for their website, which was fine by me. They gave me a brief and I delivered the shots they were after, meaning I worked on my own when I found the time. So, I made a living despite never having my head in the game. Recently, my "normal life" had taken a very serious backseat.

While nothing was going wrong, it was a good time to do some work, to get photos in while I could. Plus, aside from my images commissioned by several specific clients, I'd also taken images to sell as stock photos. Every bit counted. My work had a strong urban theme, and Chicago had some beautiful spots when the light hit it just right.

Lately, the sun had been out more. It had always been grim and overcast before. A result of pollution, everyone had said.

It took me a while to realize the gloomy days were largely because Apollo, the god of the sun and light, had rejected himself, and as he was back—love was a beautiful thing—the sun shone more. Not to mention, because he was in my life, I smiled more than I had in a long time.

I loved the outdoors, loved feeling the warmth on my face. It reminded me of Apollo's kisses. Yep, I had to catch up with him later today. Maybe with Poseidon as well. I missed him, and I couldn't believe I'd ever be so gushy over a guy... or several guys, in my case.

A warm breeze swooshed past, taking an empty chips bag with it. All the stores around me remained closed, and only the occasional car drove past.

But my mind refocused on X. I needed new weapons to give me a greater advantage in combat against him. I'd used knives, bo staffs, and nunchakus in the past, but I needed more. Every time I died, my power grew, and I became stronger. It felt as if I were being born again. Twice over, in my case. And I couldn't go back to my old ways, not after experiencing this level of power with my speed and strength. I didn't want ranged items like guns or arrows or anything cliché. Besides, I didn't get the feeling X would shy away from a bullet. A firearm was so...human. Only the power behind the weapons could beat X.

For that, I needed a melee device, something used in hand-to-hand combat. I didn't intend to use trauma items like clubs or anything similar. Instead, a daring, edgy item would work best. Maybe a different sword?

Ha. That would work wonderfully.

It'd been weeks since I last saw X or heard of the

destruction he'd caused. It wasn't that I'd forgotten about him, but I'd become a little lax. I trained hard and prepared for another fight with him, but he hadn't killed in a while. Part of me started thinking about other things again—my hopes, my dreams, the lovers in my life. The possibility of a happy future.

I checked my phone. Poseidon and Apollo sometimes messaged me, and on occasion, Ares. But nothing from Hades.

It wasn't like I was sitting on the edge of my seat waiting for him to message me or anything. But sometimes, I couldn't stop thinking about him, and I yearned to talk to him. After our last few encounters, I shouldn't have wanted anything to do with him. But he'd come to my rescue, along with the other three gods when X trapped me, and I'd never forget that moment when I realized that I wasn't alone anymore when it came to battling Death. So now, I couldn't stop hoping Hades would visit me.

But I had no idea what to think of our messed-up relationship. Who was he really? And how did he fit into this whole mess with X running around? I couldn't work it out myself, so I'd waited for him come to me. And when he hadn't, I let it go. Though he remained on my mind.

My phone pinged with a text just as I put it in my pocket, and when I unlocked the screen, I saw it was from Heracles.

Out of town. We'll train later. I'll call you when I get time.

I'd expected that, but I still sighed. I missed his company. He'd been so busy lately, going off by himself, being secretive. It wasn't how he used to be. He'd been appointed by his old man, king of the gods, Zeus, to train the Lowe family to be the protectors were born to be. But as of late, my mentor was MIA.

I stopped, leaned my back against the window of a juice store, and dialed his number. Despite him being a demigod, Heracles had a cell phone, he lived in a condo, and he wore ripped jeans and muscle tees. It was one of the things I loved him about him—he was so damn down-to-Earth.

"Are you going to avoid talking to me again?" I asked when he answered.

"Thought you might be with one of your lovers," he quipped, but there was no menace behind his words. He'd been the one who explained how gods often had multiple lovers, and the behavior was normal. That I shouldn't fight my attraction to the four gods who'd burst into my world. But at the same time, something had changed in Heracles, and he'd pulled away from me.

I forced a giggle. "Come on. Don't make fun of me. I'm starting to get this whole multiple-men thing is a part of who I am, but I'm not all the way there yet."

Heracles chuckled, and I pictured his wide smile, the creases at the corners of his eyes when he laughed.

"You haven't called me in ages," I said. "You can't just ditch our training sessions all the time. You're supposed to teach me."

"You hardly need to be taught anymore. You're as strong as I am now." A serious tone threaded his response. Was he upset my power had grown to the point where he was no longer needed?

His comment was a hell of a compliment. But I wasn't satisfied. For so long, Heracles had been all I had, the only person who understood the two worlds I straddled, whom I confided in when things got too messed up to handle on my own. And part of me felt as if I'd lost a close friend, and it was somehow my fault.

"What's been up with you?" I asked.

He hesitated, and I laughed in the silence.

"Found something better to do with your time?" I asked again, trying to get him to open up, to tell me what was going on.

"It's not that." Heracles swallowed loudly over the phone. "I love training with you. It's just...empty." His voice drifted off.

It hurt to hear him pull away, an ache settling in my gut. "Yeah, that's not an insult at all."

Heracles snickered. "I know you better than to think you bruise easily." He took a deep breath and sighed. "It's just not that easy to step down and let someone else be the hero. I'm tired of being behind the scenes. It kills me to see you fight for your life, but I can't do anything more to help you."

My gut tightened at hearing the pain in his voice, his longing to do more. "So, what? You decided not to be a hero anymore?"

"Not quite like that," he said without hesitation.

I frowned. "Are you doing…hero work?"

Heracles's laughter boomed through the phone. "We're not in a movie, Elyse. But yes. Hero work, if that's what you want to call it. I just want to feel like there's more to my life again, and there is so much crime and ugliness in this world that could use a bit of divine intervention. I've been training you Lowes for centuries. It's been great, but you're all grown up now and kicking the kind of ass I'd battle if I could. And if I'm forbidden from aiding you, I can't sit back and do nothing. A guy needs a hobby, you know?"

I smiled, understanding what he was saying. This was Heracles, the legendary hero who'd completed twelve labors. Hell, he'd defeated the Nemean Lion, captured the Erymanthian boar, and even killed the Lernean Hydra. He was the son of Zeus! So as much as it hurt to hear him following his own line of heroism, I couldn't blame him.

"Don't forget about me when you're all big and famous," I said. "And I want to meet up when you're free."

When he answered me, I heard the smile in his voice.

"I won't be famous. You'll always be my little prodigy, and you won't get rid of me that easily."

He laughed again, a deep rumble in his chest that I'd come to know and love. Heracles was like a second father to me. He'd taken over everything when I lost my family. Not just the mentoring, but he'd been the person I turned to for everything. It wasn't that I didn't need him anymore—Heracles would always be family to me. But I understood he needed more.

I could only imagine how much it exhausted him to do the same thing for centuries on end. Heracles was a better man—or god—than the rest of them put together.

After I ended the call, I pushed into a jog. But a longing danced through my chest, a feeling as if I'd somehow lost Heracles from my life. Which was ridiculous. He pulled away weeks ago, but to hear him say he was going sat on my shoulders like a boulder. I had no people in my life I considered close, and it terrified me to lose Heracles. But who was I to stop him from following his passion?

Remembering X and my mission, I decided, I'd order two blades: a katana and a scythe for good measure, once I arrived home.

I appreciated irony as much as the next person and going up to the Greek version of the Grim Reaper with a scythe sounded like pure poetry to my ears.

The weapons would be easy enough to order. With a credit card, you could do anything these days. World domination? Sure, are you paying by MasterCard or Visa? Getting these tools should have been harder, but the Lowe family had never struggled to buy them. Maybe it was a god thing. We had Zeus's special attention. I supposed it helped to have friends in high places.

After running ten blocks, I stopped and caught my breath as I adjusted my backpack, which kept getting tangled with my dark braid. My hair reached my hips, since I never cut it. After all the blood I'd gotten in it in during my last few fights, I considered cutting it to an easier length to maintain, but I didn't want to get rid of the length. My mom used to have long hair, and in a way, it reminded me of her.

This was the first time I'd grown it so long, and when I braided the hair, it was out of the way for the most part.

I flashed on an image of Hades wrapping my braid around his hand, pulling my head back so he could kiss my neck while he fucked me in the training center.

It wasn't because of him I wasn't cutting it. But God, that had been hot as hell. Everything about him left me breathless.

Which was exactly why I had to stop thinking about him—he brought trouble in more ways than one. He was my weakness and something about him drew me to him. But he was also the downfall of this Earth, from what I could see.

I didn't want to believe he was capable of something so horrific as X. But just because I didn't want it to be that way wouldn't magically make it so. I had to be realistic.

Which was why I'd stop thinking about him and get on with my day.

The streets were quiet as I passed more shopfronts. A young couple walked out of a bakery, holding hands, exchanging smiles. The man carried a bag of pastries. As much as I craved such a simple life, I refused to torture myself with what I couldn't have. I accepted I'd never have a human future, not with the power coursing through me and four gods in my life. Letting myself ponder what my future could possibly be was foolish when I wasn't even sure how I'd defeat X. And that was priority, not silly dreams of happy endings.

Soon enough, I was in a back alley, taking photos of gorgeous graffiti of an old man's head with fish swimming out of his ears that a nameless street artist had spray painted on an old brick building. While I had no clue what it meant, as long as it made sense to the artist that was what mattered.

A sudden cloud of darkness surrounded me.

My heart raced. I stumbled and caught myself on the wall. This fog didn't feel like X. The darkness seemed as if it were inside of me, resonating with something familiar, and I swallowed hard, trying to stay awake and on my feet. Heaviness sank through my body, the sensation growing denser inside me, almost dragging me under. I scanned the alley on either side of me. No sign of anyone else.

Energy hummed over my flesh, calling me, and fear bubbled in my chest. The kind that screamed to *fight*!

After dying twice, the increasing darkness inside me was one side effect I worried about. I had a strength and awesome energy, sure. But it was as if a little piece of myself disappeared every time I died, replaced by the new power that clung to my insides. It was like being unable to take a deep enough breath, no matter how much I tried.

This wasn't X, but me, and whatever was happening to me after my last death.

I could only die one more time and wake up again, or would the drowning feeling drag me to a darkness I'd never wake up from instead?

The thought terrified me. After my father died, it had almost killed me to lose him. But I always I held on to the promise I'd spend time with him again one day in the afterworld. Except if X took my life, I'd never get a chance to see Dad; I would perish from existence. And not even the gods could do a damn thing to save me.

A while ago, I thought my ability to come back to life was a bonus. I'd been damn flippant about it, especially when I'd killed myself so quickly to escape X. I'd done it to survive, for more power, and I'd gotten it. But I regretted killing myself now, wasting a life when I could have waited for the gods to come and help me.

But it was too late for hindsight. And what was it they said about spilled milk? Better to look forward and to focus on what came next.

To that end, I kept my eyes peeled for X in case he

appeared. Usually, where there was darkness, he followed. And Hades was often not far behind. The whole idea tore me apart because the feelings growing inside me for Hades were the opposite of the hatred I held for X. That bastard had shown me a vision where he killed my father, and I trembled at the memory. Bile hit the back of my throat. Fuck, I knew it hadn't been real, but the ass had played with my mind, and I wanted to drive my sword deep into his black heart.

So, was Hades the one who'd set X free? And if he had, what were his reasons? Or had X somehow escaped from Hades and all this chaos was out of Hades's control?

I wanted to believe the latter. But that would mean I trusted Hades. And despite being attracted to him, I wasn't sure I could fully trust him. I didn't want to see him as a villain, but everyone else seemed to. And he did have that devil-may-care attitude, even when it came to the deaths of the humans X killed before their time came.

If Hades wasn't behind this, why didn't he try to stop X?

My breaths caught in my chest, and I exhaled slowly, needing to release the growing anxiety. Along with the fear I'd discover Hades was the bad guy after all and I'd let myself fall for him.

I wanted to believe he was a hero like the rest of us, but I was too scared he'd prove me wrong again. He was already volatile, and I never knew what to expect from him. I couldn't discount that he could be the one behind the darkness that brewed in the heart of Chicago.

Because with Hades, it was impossible to know how quickly the weather would change.

CHAPTER 2

Elyse

*A*fter a couple of hours of photography, I finished and headed home. Yet my mind remained on Hades and on X, even when taking photos and trying to find the right shots for my clients. I stepped out of the alleyway just as movement caught my attention in my peripheral vision. I turned to find a dead pigeon on its back, near a dumpster. I glanced up and studied the busy sidewalk, but nothing seemed out of the ordinary. Poor bird. It must have been its time. Unlike the people X had taken before their deaths.

The earlier unease lingered, while a coldness swirled around my legs, yet the wind remained distant. My mind replayed a short loop of him jumping me not long ago when I hadn't expected him. The gods came to my rescue, but it was a reminder to always remain vigilant.

Where are you, X? I swallowed hard, hating this cat-and-mouse game. What the fuck was he waiting for? My stomach heaved, and each step I took through the crowds felt like a move toward my own grave. Everything in my mind tumbled around X.

My phone buzzed, and I flinched. *Fuck*, the asshole had me high-strung. I collected the phone from my pocket and answered it.

"What are you doing?" Catina asked.

I exhaled and let my muscles untangle. Hearing from my simple, straightforward human friend was a welcome break from everything. It was a rarity in my life these days; plus, she offered me the distraction I needed from my hectic otherworldly business.

Recently, though, Catina and I hadn't been as close as we used to be. Even when I saw her at *Foundation*, the magazine that had me on retainer for some fashion but mostly city life photos, it just wasn't the same.

Every time I learned more about my role as a godly fighter, the more I felt like Catina and I were drawing away from each other. Plus, she didn't see eye to eye with me on my choice of lovers...more specifically, with how many I had.

But I missed my friend—it was an ache that came and went, sitting in my gut like a slow-burning fire, always returning in quiet moments. I missed how around her, everything felt easy and there wasn't anything to worry about other than looking good on our nights out and whether some guy was a good kisser or not. God, those days seemed a lifetime away. I wanted to hear her gossip about work, to laugh at funny things she did, and to enjoy her company... But if I let myself dwell on what was slipping away, I'd crumble.

"I'm working," I said. "Got some amazing photos of the city."

"That's new," she replied with a smile in her voice, and I breathed easy.

I'd been uncertain how things would play out between us after our last argument. Especially since Catina wouldn't let go of her viewpoint, so we agreed not to talk about her disapproval over my love life and try to make our friendship work. To somehow return to where we used to be.

I laughed because she was right, I didn't often work. Not as frequently as I trained. Or fought.

"Why?" I asked, slightly hesitant. "What's up?"

"I got off work early today. Do you want to meet up?"

Was she wanting another serious conversation over how many men I dated? Or was I overreacting?

Yet, she carried a cheery tone behind her words. This was what I missed, my friend laughing and catching up, so I agreed. I longed to see her, rekindle our friendship, and spend time with her doing the little things that didn't matter but made me feel so good. I needed to know we were both moving forward and attempting to make our relationship work.

We met at the Metric Coffee Co., as usual. It was her favorite place. Even though I didn't love coffee that much, the artisan shop had become the place I associated with Catina and a good time.

When I hugged her hello. Her hair hung longer than usual—she always looked stunning, no matter how long she wore her blonde hair. But it was a testament to how little time we spent together.

"I feel like we hardly talk anymore," Catina said after we'd ordered our coffee and sat down at one of the tables.

"I've been so busy." I fidgeted with my fingernails.

Catina nodded but didn't answer me. I half-expected her to ask what I was so busy with, to mention the men in my life. I didn't want to keep lying to her, but there was a very blurry line between the truth of what I was doing and insanity.

It'd been a while since Catina and I spent time together without fighting. The past couple of months had been weird for me. I developed feelings for at least three different men, and I still had to smooth things out with the one guy, Poseidon, whom Catina thought was solid.

Then there was Oliver, my neighbor. To be fair, he was a great guy. And he'd make some ordinary girl extremely happy. But it just wouldn't work for me. Oliver had a crush on me for a long time, and we'd gotten as far as organizing a date before I stood him up. But we'd mostly eased over that awkward situation.

I hated that I hurt him in the process, but it was better this way because he and I could never work out. And I had enough men in my life.

"So, how's your love life?" Catina asked.

I glanced at her warily. And there it was, *the* question. We'd gotten stuck on the men in my life. She didn't agree with my polyamorous life, which was what this was becoming.

"It's fine." I shrugged.

"You're still with…what was his name? Al?"

"Yeah."

"And Phil?" The bridge of her nose creased slightly, as if she struggled to say the name and admit I was with more than one guy. But when she smiled, her brow smoothed over.

God, those names. I cringed that I'd given the God of the Seas and the God of Music and Light silly names like "Al" and "Phil," but what was I supposed to do? Tell Catina their real names? She'd ask a dozen questions, and I hated that I'd already lied to her.

"Yeah." I glanced at my friend, waiting for her reaction. Judgment, a fight—this was what had happened before.

She looked at me, and for a moment, it could have gone either way. But then she nodded and took a sip of her coffee.

"And how is that going?" she asked without a hint of criticism. No raised brow or glare.

When I didn't respond, she continued, "Hey, I know we fought last time we spoke, but I want to be friends and I'm sorry, your love life is none of my business. I worry about you. You're my best friend, and I guess dating multiple guys took me by surprise."

The tension building around us died down as if the atmosphere was holding its breath, then it finally let it out again.

"It's going okay. I mean, they're both great." I smiled at her, still a little unsure how she was going to respond.

And Catina seemed just as careful and standoffish. We were both testing the waters. But I made a decision after our last argument that I wasn't going to hide who I was anymore, no matter what. And apparently, she'd accepted whatever it was going on with me. Plus, I appreciated her apology to clear the air.

What a friend, and I meant whole-heartedly.

"Are those the only two you're interested in?" she asked, taking a sip of her coffee.

I wasn't sure if she was being sarcastic. But when I studied her, her face was open, her expression curious. She really wanted to know. I had my guard up, expecting her to attack, and it felt amazing when she didn't.

Even if the boys we were talking about were gods. And there was more than one love in my life.

"It's complicated." I turned my coffee cup around and around on the table, feeling a little silly to tell her about Hades and the new addition of Ares on my radar.

"Why?" she asked, her eyes focused on me, as she gave her full attention.

I shrugged. "I'm not sure if this one guy…Harry…is an ass or not. I mean, I can't stay away from him. But he might not be a very good guy."

"Does he treat you badly?" Her voice deepened, taking on a serious tone.

God, if I thought back to the sex we'd had, then no, he didn't treat me badly at all. But the rest of it? X and how Hades was with me sometimes when he was in a bad mood?

"He's just hard to figure out," I said, unsure how to explain when I didn't fully comprehend him myself. Hades tore me in opposite directions as my brain and body had entirely different ideas about him.

She looked down at the table, tracing a scratch with her fingernails. "Can I ask you something?" she queried hesitantly.

"Sure." I grew wary of her questions, but I wasn't going to push this away. She was trying, so it would only be fair if I tried, too.

"Are these guys all okay with each other? I mean, you have more than one, but do they know? You're not going to get into some kind of trouble?"

I smiled at her and reached over, to pat her hand.

"They know about each other. I'm not hiding them from one another."

"And they're fine with it?" One of her brows arched as she studied me.

I shrugged again. "They haven't told me otherwise." Poseidon and Hades weren't on the best footing, but history explained that perfectly. It had nothing to do with dating me. And the others? Apollo and Poseidon were totally cool with each other.

And even though I liked Ares, he wasn't exactly part of the group when it came down to anything, never mind whatever was going on between us.

If I had to be honest, I hadn't even thought about what they'd think of each other, and how they'd all feel about having to share me. I supposed it showed exactly how accepting everyone was because there hadn't been a single fight over me, as far as I knew.

Who could have thought men would be this reasonable? Then again, they were all gods. The normal rules didn't apply to them. Or to me, for that matter. Something that took some getting used to.

"I'm sort of starting to see why you're not interested in Oliver." Her words lulled me out of my thoughts, but her comment came out of the blue. The poor guy found me when I'd killed myself to avoid X. Heracles took care of him, scrubbed his memories or something. And we were friends again, although our friendship was a little weird now. It was as if he still knew something was up but couldn't remember.

21

Not consciously.

I hadn't talked to him in a few weeks. Even though he lived next door and we often passed each other coming or going.

"He's a great guy," I said. "He's just not the guy for me."

Catina nodded and stared into the distance momentarily as if caught in her own fantasy. "I think whoever he dates, he'll treat like a queen. She'd have no questions about his intentions toward her."

I nodded. She was right, it would be way simpler to be with Oliver. But I couldn't be with him when there was so much in my life I couldn't talk to him about. And I couldn't fall in love with a man when I wasn't drawn to him. I'd never been attracted to Oliver, not even in the normal sense of the word.

And definitely not in the way I was pulled to the gods. There was something about them, about their magic, that drew me. Maybe the answer lay in the power within me that responded to theirs. Or maybe I hadn't ever been like the rest of the human girls. Because the blood that pumped through my veins was infused with godlike power—the small blessing Zeus had bestowed on the Lowe bloodline.

"Why are you so serious about Oliver?" I asked.

When I'd allowed Oliver to take me on a date, Heracles had come to get me to fight X, and I'd ditched Oliver to save the world. What a bitch I was.

"He's a nice guy, Elyse," she replied. "Just saying."

I straightened my posture, not loving her pushiness. "Then why don't you date him?"

It came out a little snappy, and she lowered her gaze, subdued. Normally, she'd have fought back. She really was trying.

"Maybe I will," she murmured so softly I barely heard her. But I was pretty sure she'd said the words. "Would that be okay with you?"

"Yes, of course. You have my blessing." I'd never heard her speak of Oliver in any way that indicated she might have been interested in him. Or had I missed the clues, too preoccupied with my own world?

She glanced up at me, and I couldn't tell what she was thinking. Was she being sarcastic or honest? But her cheeks glowed.

"I have to get going," she said, glancing at the clock on the wall. "Will I see you in the office anytime soon?"

"Yeah, I think Tina wants me in again soon. I'll look you up."

Catina nodded and started telling me about a project she was working on. The conversation had returned to girly and uncomplicated. I grinned and nodded and let her guide the conversation wherever she was comfortable.

It was the least I could do, though I kept wondering about her and Oliver. Had I missed something all this time and she'd had a thing for him? Why wouldn't she tell me before? Or was she testing the waters before she made a move on him? They had my blessing if that was the case.

When it was time to go, Catina hugged me, holding me longer than usual, as if she'd wanted more time together as well.

"Thanks for this," she said with a kindness in her smile, a gentleness because she was the kind of person who lived how she believed people should. With her heart on her sleeve. "I needed our catch up."

I nodded. "Always. I'll see you soon." To those around us, we probably seemed like two close friends, chatting about casual things, but we both knew why there was a strain in our relationship.

She walked away first, and I watched her climb into her car before I strolled over to mine. Regular coffee time with her was a must. I'd come to the conclusion that my life would always be hectic and chaotic, so I'd make time to mend the rifts.

The conversation had been a little tense, but not because of a pending fight. Rather, it was because, in some ways, we were strangers. So much had happened lately, and we needed to find our place together again.

But in other ways, Catina was still my best friend from school, the only one willing to be my friend and pull me into her circle. And I loved her dearly for always being by my side as I'd grown up.

I was relieved our friendship hadn't dissolved. We'd do what we'd always done; focus on the little things, because she was the only one who allowed me to feel normal. She meant so much more to me than she'd ever understand.

The branches of the oak tree I'd parked near stopped swaying and fell to a deadly silence. Coldness lingered around me. The smell of the city in the air shifted from the aroma of car pollution, brewed coffee, and the fresh smell of cut grass to something else. An electric scent. It tingled over my arms, lifting the hairs. The world around me fell quiet, no cars driving past, the people at the café seemed too quiet, and the sky was clear with the exception of a plane flying overhead. Everything seemed normal, but it didn't feel right. The earlier darkness surged through me, burrowing in my chest.

My pulse raced, and I scanned the location. There was no sign of X, and like the alleyway, that heaviness in the air returned, pressing against me. I climbed into my car and drove away, checking my mirrors, unable to shake off that sensation of being watched.

CHAPTER 3

Ares

I arrived at the training center on Tuesday in my workout clothes—sweats and a T-shirt that I'd get to throw off once I started practicing. I shoved on the wraparound sunglasses I'd bought at a store for a ridiculous amount of money because they made me look good.

And I liked them. I enjoyed being the badass, the cool guy, the man all the girls stared at when they strolled past me. If I really intended to, I could get so much ass down here.

But there was only one ass that held my interest and she flooded my thoughts.

Saying it that way made me sound like a dick. The truth was, Elyse was more than just a piece of ass. Although that body of hers was a fucking orgasm waiting to happen. But she was someone who cared about others and who'd stick it out when shit got tough.

There weren't a lot of those kinds of people or gods around. And even though the other gods thought I was a coward who didn't bother what the fuck was going on, I cared. Elyse and I had a hell of a lot more in common than she'd admit.

Which made me even more interested in spending time with her, discovering who she really was, and what I could do to bring out her smile.

When Heracles called and asked me to step in to help her practice fighting, I'd jumped at the chance. Even if it was none of my business where she worked out and why. Zeus was the one who gave Heracles the job of training Elyse and her family, but I'd do anything if someone explained she needed me. Pathetic, but true. This was my chance to show her the real me.

Besides, Heracles said that I was the best fighter of the lot, and he wanted me on the case. A little ego stroking never hurt anyone.

Elyse was growing strong. I hadn't seen her before she died that first time. I'd only come toward the end to help out because Heracles had asked Zeus for backup. And the fucker sent me. Maybe it was some sick joke, and it pissed me off.

But now I was glad he had. Because I'd seen her fight and she was as lethal as she was hot. A real femme fatale. And after she killed herself to outsmart X, dying a second time, her power intensified again. I hadn't seen her in action yet, not against anyone who mattered. But if the rumors about her family were true —and it looked like they were—she'd practically be hell on wheels right now.

And I wanted a piece of that. Hell, I craved her. I was the God of War and being able to fight, having that skill and putting it to use to help others, was the kind of thing a man like me craved in a woman.

I couldn't remember the last time I'd actually desired a certain woman this much. And not just for sex, but for more. Until now, it had been all about having a fucking good time.

Pun intended.

But love? No thanks. Only someone like Elyse might change my mind.

She was already at the training center when I arrived, her car parked in the dark lot. I spotted two dead pigeons nearby. Fuck, Chicago was infested with those things. The sun hadn't risen yet, night still hung thick in the air, and it was that rare time of morning when people from the night shift and those getting ready for the day shift actually crossed paths.

Elyse was dressed in pants so tight they looked painted on and a top that barely covered her breasts, keeping her strapped in. Her rock-hard abs and her sculpted arms showed, her skin pale and perfect. Her hair was back in a braid, swinging from side to side as she used the jump rope, warming up. There was power in her hair. I didn't have to touch it to know that.

Everything about this woman was riddled with magic that drew me in like a magnet. I was attracted to her with a kind of heady trance that drew bees to nectar. She was a reliable person whom I'd trust to watch my back. Not many gained that status in my book. I yearned to stare into her chocolate eyes and run my hands over her soft skin.

I watched her for a while before announcing myself. Her body jiggled while she jumped, but there wasn't much excess fat on her. It was muscle trembling as she exerted herself, pushing harder and harder.

I'd tap that. Any day. In fact, I nearly had.

We'd fought, Elyse and I. At first, we sparred. But there'd been anger, both from my side and hers. And then the fiery lust had grown from anger and our close contact. Her lips had tasted like sweat and I sensed her desire for me. I'd been more than happy to oblige.

She'd stopped herself, and I respected her, so I stopped too.

But God, I'd dreamed about that moment so many times. My body ached for more—my dick twitched with need. I could have gone out there and found some human to fuck every time I thought about her and fulfill the need. But I didn't.

Elyse deserved more than that. Even if it wasn't like I owed her any kind of exclusivity. We were fellow warriors. Nothing more.

Yet I didn't want to do something filthy when she was so pure. She was the embodiment of everything good in the world.

Cliché? Absolutely.

I'd give Apollo's poetry a run for its money if I allowed myself to get serious about what I thought of Elyse. And I'd stared at her long enough, so I cleared my throat. She didn't hear me, too caught up in what she was doing, focusing on her form, no doubt high on the adrenaline that ran through her system. I knew what that felt like. Heart pumping, lungs bursting, and muscles screaming for more.

So, to announce myself, I walked around to approach her from the front.

She stopped jumping, breathing hard, her surprised face morphing into a frown at seeing me. The rope hung limply to the ground.

"What are you doing here?" she panted, catching her breath. Sweat beaded down the sides of her neck.

"I'm here to train with you." I hooked my thumbs into the sweatpants' pockets. "I even dressed the part."

A small smile played on her lips, but her eyes were serious. Dark eyes. Drowning deep. The type of eyes I wanted to fall into if I could.

Fuck! I was getting emotional and corny as well.

"I didn't realize you did anything that wasn't for yourself," she said with a sneer.

The words had been spoken in jest, and I understood she was just playing, but they stung. Everyone thought I was a deserter, a coward—but they were all wrong. I could do shit for the greater good, too. But no one seemed to believe me.

"Don't do that," I cautioned instead of laughing it off like I always did or making some stupid joke in return.

"What?" she asked, the smile slipping away from her lips.

"Don't mock me. You don't know me." I removed my shades and tucked them into my pocket.

She nodded. "You're right. I don't."

No apology. But it wasn't like Elyse to grovel. It wouldn't have been hot if she had. But she seemed to get what I felt anyway.

"Are we training together or what?" I questioned when the silence stretched out.

She thought about it for a moment then grinned a dazzling smile that lit up her features. Fuck me, she was beautiful.

"Yeah, let's see if you can keep up." She smirked as if challenging me.

Bring it on. I nodded and pulled off my shirt. When I dropped it on the floor, her gaze slid over my torso, and her lips parted slightly.

Well, didn't that just make me feel like a stud? I jumped up and down on the spot to warm up, too. *Let's do this.*

We trained together afterward. When she made the comment about me keeping up, I'd thought she was being cocky. Talking smack and all that. But she'd been serious. She was fucking fit, and she trained hard.

After doing weights, we moved on to sparring. We worked on hand-to-hand combat. It was her favorite, she explained.

"Why?" I asked. "Don't humans prefer weapons?"

Elyse laughed. "I guess they do. But I'm not an ordinary human, am I?"

"No," I agreed, my gaze falling to her flawlessly sculpted lips. They glistened with sweat, and I thought back to how delicious they tasted, wondering if her pussy was the same color.

"Besides, X isn't a normal adversary either." Her voice cut through my focus on her mouth. "If not for our family bloodline being blessed, I'd have never gotten this far."

"It's not just Zeus's power," I said. "You have a lot of talent."

She laughed again. "Are you trying to flirt with me?"

"If I was trying to flirt with you, you wouldn't have to ask." Grinning, I slid my gaze over her body, taking in every delicious inch of her. And she blushed. Like a teenager. Holy fuck, that turned me on.

"Let's up the ante," she suggested.

"What?" I was still thinking about sex, and I was unsure what she meant.

But she showed me. She moved faster than a human should have been able to move and hit me in the chest with a kick that sent me backward, and nearly winded me.

"That's new." I coughed, filling my lungs with air, stunned by her ability.

"Yeah."

I didn't let her explain further. I retaliated, launching at her with the same speed—a tempo that should only have belonged to the gods. But she was ready for me, blocking my punch and striking out, planting a knee in my side. I grunted and quit holding back.

We were still just sparring, not fighting all-out. But if this was how hard she fought when training, I could only imagine what a force she'd be on the battlefield. She'd become so much stronger than I'd realized after her second death.

She didn't give me a chance to think about what was happening, and I did what I did best. I fought. Fists flew, blows were blocked, I kicked, and she jumped back. She attacked, and I parried. Her braid flew through the air when she spun around and twice I tried to grab for it. But despite having a weakness like that, she knew how to keep her hair out of my hands.

When we finally paused for a break, we both breathed hard, sweating like animals, and Elyse's eyes glittered with adrenaline and the thrill of the fight. Her cheeks were flushed, and strands of flyaway hair had escaped from her braid.

She looked fucking fantastic.

"Don't you get tired of doing all this?" I asked as we sat side by side on the floor, draining our water bottles.

She tilted her head from side to side, as if weighing her choices. "It's what I was born to do. The people need me."

"You never wished for something different?" I probed, glancing down at her forearm where X had bitten her. Where her skin was lined with black marks from the injury. It had definitely improved from when he'd first bitten her and it had looked like her skin was rotting.

"Sometimes, but there's no one else left to do this. It's who I am, how my dad brought me up. It's for the greater good, right?"

Was that sarcasm in her voice? Had she ever thought about kids? Or had she made up her mind about what having them would mean—subjecting those she loved to her lifestyle? To the way her father had brought her up? She'd watched her family die after all. Yet, without their bloodline, the world would be doomed. And if she decided on having children, who would she ask to father her baby? Part of me was convinced that if she looked at me in the right way, I wouldn't say no right away. I'd need time to think about the implications. But in truth, I didn't know if a god could father children with a Lowe.

Fuck, all those thoughts hurt my head.

I nodded in response to her comment. "I can understand that."

Elyse frowned. "Really?"

"Yeah." I turned to face her. "Everyone thinks I'm selfish and a coward and all the other shit. But I'm the God of War. And there is no war without a cause. I care about who gets hurt and why. There's so much fucked-up crap out there. And not just these days, either. It's always been like that."

She stared at me for a long time with a strange look on her face. Compassion?

"You're right," she finally admitted.

"About what?"

"What you said earlier. I don't know you. At all."

The atmosphere shifted between us, charging with that same power I'd felt before. It was her magic and my energy, plus some kind of pull that made me think we'd fit together if we tried.

I leaned forward until her face was mere inches from mine. Her breath caught in her throat, but she didn't pull away. Instead, her eyes slid to my lips.

I kissed her before I could stop myself. And she kissed me back this time, parting her lips for me to taste her. Sweet heaven, she intoxicated me, and I breathed in her sexy scent. She arched, her soft breasts pressed against my chest, and I drew her closer. One kiss, and I was lost, just like our first time. Electricity pricked my skin, and fuck, she had me craving her with such intensity.

My body was on fire, heat dancing on my skin, my nerve endings alive. I put my hand on her jaw, my fingers brushing against her neck, and magic poured between the two of us, more powerful than any we'd experienced before. Stronger than anything I'd ever sensed with a lover.

And that was exactly what I wanted from Elyse. To be her lover. Not just to fuck, but something deeper.

Hell! What was she doing to me?

I wasn't sure I really cared.

CHAPTER 4

Elyse

On Thursday, just as I was wrapping up a workout, I received a text from Catina.

Drinks tonight?

We hadn't done the nightclub scene in a while. I'd never been a big drinker since it numbed my senses and I couldn't feel what was going on around me. At the moment, I needed to be ready for when X attacked, not letting my guard down.

But for the sake of my friendship with Catina, I could make an exception of going out with her and not getting drunk. Plus, with my new power, I had no idea of my limit was when it came to alcohol, so I wouldn't push it.

I called her instead of texting her back. "Can I come

over now? I just finished with training, and you're on the way home."

She giggled. "You've got such a chill life. Working out, some photos, and a hell of a lot of sleep. What a way to live it up."

I chuckled. Not because it was funny, but because she couldn't be more wrong. What I wouldn't give to not look over my shoulder at every shadow. To not worry about being attacked again or how I might be too late to stop him from killing. But X hadn't murdered any innocents lately. I couldn't sense him and neither could the gods. Why he remained hidden and silent baffled me. Maybe Hades had regained control? Something I'd have to find out later.

Catina's breath danced on the other side of the phone, bringing me back to the present.

"What can I say?" I told her. "I was chosen for this kind of lifestyle." I smiled at the truth. I *had* been chosen, and my dad and brothers brought me up reminding me of this fact every single day. To never take our abilities for granted. Zeus had selected our family to protect humans against monsters, and the responsibility had been passed on to me. I didn't intend to let Dad down by not continuing in his footsteps.

"Come over when you're ready. I just got home," Catina said.

I loaded my duffel bag in my car, and it clanged, metal hitting metal. My new swords had arrived, and I'd practiced with them today. But my thoughts sailed to one of my workouts with Ares from two days ago, the way we'd fought without restraint and he'd pushed me further. Then there was our kiss, and my lips tingled in memory. Part of me burst to tell someone how I felt, but thinking about seeing him again was ridiculous. Didn't I have enough gods in my life?

Anyway, I still had a bit of work to do using the new weapons, but I already loved the way the blades sang when I sliced them through the air.

I hadn't tried out my scythe yet. All in good time.

When I arrived at Catina's place, she opened the door with a glass of white wine in her hand.

"Just in time." She lifted the glass to me in a salute.

I smiled, adoring her laidback attitude. "I won't hug you. I'm sweaty." I was still in my Lycra pants, tank top, and sneakers, as they were comfortable for fighting. Any other time I was in jeans or leather. While I owned a pair of heels, I couldn't remember the last time I wore them.

She laughed. "Some things never change. Wine?"

I declined the offer of alcohol. "Not until we go out later at least. I can't drink right after training. I'm sure there's a rule against that."

"Only in your book," she said with a grin.

I stepped into her apartment and sat on the couch. Catina joined me, folding her feet underneath her and taking a sip of wine. It was great to be here again, to feel as if I had somewhere I belonged aside from my own place.

"That's new." I pointed to a large painting above her mantel.

Catina nodded. "I spoiled myself. I've wanted to buy something for the apartment forever. So, I did. Why not?"

"I agree; it's good to spoil yourself once in a while." Yet I couldn't remember the last time I had. Buying weapons online wasn't exactly spoiling myself.

I studied the painting—an abstract thing of a sapphire wave moving along the canvas. Not my style at all, but it had Catina written all over it.

"Any news?" she questioned, taking another drink of her wine.

"Like what?" I asked.

"I don't know. My life is so run-of-the-mill." She slouched on the sofa. "Tell me gossip, some excitement. Your life is anything but ordinary."

I chuckled. She was right, but what could I tell her? I thought about Ares. "I met this guy."

She rolled her eyes. "God, another one?"

I bit my cheek. I refused to tell her if she was going to judge me. I wasn't here for that.

"Sorry." She straightened her posture, as if sensing my reaction. "That came out wrong. It just feels like I hardly know you lately. All these men, and them accepting you having multiple lovers and whatever. It's confusing."

I pulled up my shoulders without answering. What could I say?

"But tell me," she insisted. "I'll pretend he's the only one there is and try to give you advice. What are friends for?"

I smiled, ready to give this a go. Catina really was great and I appreciated her trying. "Okay, so I've known him for a while. We have some stuff in common, like training. He puts on such a big act, though. But I get the feeling he's totally different under the bravado. And I'm starting to like him."

"So, do you want to know if you should go for him?" she asked, tilting her head as she studied me.

"Something like that. There's this crazy attraction with him. But at the same time, he's unpredictable. And I don't need that right now." My life was one great ball of uncertainty at the moment.

She smirked and took another sip. "I'll bet."

I smiled because it was hilarious when I looked at it from an outsider's perspective. And I got the sense she wasn't making fun of me this time.

"It'd be cliché if I told you to follow your heart, huh?" she queried.

"A little."

"Get to know him, then," she suggested. "But you guys have training in common, which you practically live for, so that should be fun."

I laughed again, remembering our workout session. It'd been spectacular. Ares was great to spar with. He was as serious about his fighting as I was and where Heracles always taught me the right way to move and block, Ares fought me like a worthy opponent. With him, there was no thinking. Only action.

And then there was our kiss. The way he'd stared at me so intensely, his passion flooding me, and he hadn't pushed me to go further than a kiss, as if waiting for me to make the next move. Something about that made me respect him. Yet it left me craving him and yep, I'd lost myself to him in that moment. God, he adored me beyond physical attraction! How was I supposed to fight against such thoughts? I could swear his musky smell flooded my senses right now, his strong hands holding me close, the play of his tongue against mine, and our racing breaths.

I glanced over at Catina, who was still drinking her wine and seemed to be genuinely contemplating what to do about Ares. Not only to find an answer for me, but to accept my life and to give us a chance.

"Are you seriously considering dating Oliver?" I asked, curious where her love life was going and remembering our last conversation about him at Metric Coffee Co.

She snapped her head up to me, her cheeks on fire. "What are you talking about?"

I giggled. "You're not a convincing liar. Don't pretend you don't know. You said you'd date him if I didn't and asked if I was okay with it."

She turned a darker shade of crimson, and I shifted on the couch with discomfort. I hadn't meant to make her blush. If she liked the guy, she ought to just say it.

"He doesn't even like me," she blurted out, and then she was on her feet. She marched over to the mantel, where she lit a candle, the scent of vanilla reaching me. Outside, a car honked, and a silence fell between us.

"What if you just get to know him?" I echoed her own words back to her.

She laughed that time as she joined me on the couch again. "Thanks, Elyse. You're a peach."

We giggled together, and it felt amazing. I could actually see Catina with Oliver, which would have seemed bizarre at first. But it'd work. They were both human, which was a huge bonus. Both were driven. He was gentle and accepting and supportive. And she was wild and free and in need of a solid foundation.

Perfect match.

While we talked, I became aware of a shift in the atmosphere in her apartment, and my skin prickled. The room was growing darker, as if the clouds had moved in front of the sun. Yet the sun was still out.

"Do you feel that?" I asked Catina.

"What?" She glanced around, then back at me, and shrugged.

Of course she couldn't feel the oppressive sensation, as it was the same one that lay inside of me. It had its roots in magic and power from another dimension, and Catina was just a human.

But I recognized the darkness. It burrowed under my skin, sped up my pulse, and was different than what

I'd felt in the alleyway. I stiffened in my seat, well aware of what was coming.

X.

Why was he looking for me here when he'd been nowhere to be seen for weeks?

But that was all over, wasn't it? X had returned to fight me. And when we fought, he didn't care about the souls that became collateral. Not that he ever cared, but this time, I cared more than usual.

I couldn't let anything happen to Catina. I jumped up, my heart racing, and ran to one of the windows to look out. The street and apartment buildings outside seemed normal, but the darkness in the air that felt like a black fog. I turned as mist curled around my feet with a chill, filling the apartment like a twisted smoke machine.

"What's going on?" Catina inquired, her voice shaky, obviously still oblivious to what was happening. But how could she know? If she did, she'd be screaming and running for her life.

"He's here," I breathed.

"Who?" She hugged one of the couch pillows to her chest, staring at me as if I'd gone mad. "You're scaring me."

X appeared inside the apartment out of thin air. Dread pushed against me like an invisible gale, and I locked my jaw tight, my muscles tense.

The fuckhead looked about as human as he ever would, but there was nothing about him that wasn't short of a nightmare. His smooth, dark skin stretched across his body, while his eyes burned like an eternal fire. His pupils were never-ending pits of doom, and I instinctively looked away from his eyes.

Catina screamed, and I flinched. X had made himself visible to her—he very often stayed out of the humans' way. But today, he was the bogeyman, the monster under the bed that was real. And the world seemed to freeze in those few moments when reality crashed through me, my heart ticking like a bomb in my chest.

"Elyse, what the fuck is that?" Catina yelled, spilling her wine over her pants and couch. She whimpered, hysterically crawling backward on the couch, and jumped off to put distance between her and X.

"Get out of here. Run!" I wasn't taking the time to explain. X was in my territory now, and he was going to get what was coming to him. I was stronger and faster than ever, and I could take him.

I used my newfound speed, shooting from the one side of the room to the other so that I stood right in front of X in a blur. I struck out at him with a fist, aiming for his jaw. And the blow would have been perfect if he hadn't been anticipating an attack.

But somehow, X wasn't there for me, even though I had thought he was initially. Instead of fighting or even blocking my blows and kicks, he merely sidestepped me as if I were inconsequential. He gave me a smile that flashed sharp fangs, and like a vision, he disappeared from my side of the room and reappeared in front of Catina.

A chill crawled over me, numbing my brain.

Catina stood paralyzed with fear. She trembled on the spot, looking up at X. All the blood drained from her face.

"Don't look into his eyes!" I shouted, but it was too late. The expression on Catina's face sank as she fell, fell, fell.

My brain only offered me one thought: this was it. This was where I'd watch my best friend die. Lead seemed to fill my stomach, and my feet were set in concrete. They shouldn't have been, but panic slithered through me.

X had started sucking the souls out of his victims instead of sending them to the Underworld, consuming them and adding them to his arsenal of magic. He was going to use my friend the same way he'd used so many other humans he'd consumed.

"Catina," I cried out, charging X. I threw a punch against the side of his head, but my fist flew right through his form. He was fading, the darkness of his body becoming transparent enough for me to see Catina through him. Her eyes were wide, rolling in their sockets and her expression was riddled with the knowledge of her death.

My stomach dropped, and fear slammed into me, ragged and harsh.

But X didn't consume my friend as I expected him

to. He disappeared the moment I reached out a hand to grab him.

"Catina!"

But by then, she was gone, too. X had taken her. Why hadn't he consumed her when he had the chance? He never took victims away to kill them. Was this a hostage situation? As scared as I was for Catina, it was almost too good to be true. It meant I had a freaking chance to save my friend.

The spot where Catina had stood only moments before was empty, every sliver of darkness dissolved, the apartment undisturbed as if nothing had happened. I remained alone in the middle of the room, panic creeping up on me.

I fumbled for my phone in my pocket and called the first number on my list: Apollo.

"He took her," I mumbled, hysterics wracking my body as I started hyperventilating. My breath refused to enter my lungs, and the room tilted beneath me.

"Elyse, calm down," Apollo demanded. "Who took her? Who got taken?"

"X." I swallowed hard and barely got the words out. "The fucker took Catina. And he didn't kill her."

Apollo was quiet for only a second, so I rattled off Catina's address, talking over him.

"I'll be right there, then take you home straight away," he said, and the line went dead.

CHAPTER 5

Ares

*E*ven though the situation was dire, I couldn't help but enjoy the glimpse into Elyse's personal life while in her apartment. We all rushed here after Apollo let us know he'd taken her home.

The framed photos on the television stand drew my attention, especially the one with a young Elyse standing next to a woman with the same chestnut-colored hair. Had to be her mom, but I'd heard from the others her mother had passed away as well. And staring at the joy on her face in the photo reminded me of sorrow. Was that how she felt each time she looked at the image? Remembering happier days now lost forever?

I'd only truly loved once. Aphrodite had been my life, but after the fucked-up stunt her husband,

Hephaestus, had pulled, humiliating us by catching us in a net on his bed, I'd refused to ever fall for another so deeply again. I should have rained down a war on Hephaestus, but shit, I'd been the god sleeping with his wife. Fuck, I'd loved her so much, and it took me centuries to get over her. Throwing myself into combat and wars gave me the distraction I'd needed to deal with the loss.

Yet since arriving in Chicago, I'd found myself drawn to Elyse, and those familiar feelings rose through me. She reminded me so much of myself. Full of anger, jumping into any situation rather than thinking it through, and just wanting to be accepted. It was so obvious she struggled to fit into the human world because she wasn't a mortal.

While I might have desired a peek into who she really was, there were much bigger things at hand. I wasn't going to be the dick who didn't care about someone Elyse had lost.

She sat on the black couch with a cup of coffee Poseidon had made. She wasn't exactly rocking back and forth, but she was paler than usual. Plus, I caught the slight tremble of her hands.

And understandably so. Her best friend had just been kidnapped by X.

This stunt was new for Thanatos—Death—X—whatever the fuck he was called. This guy seemed to pull a new trick out of his sleeve at every turn. First, it was killing humans without Hades's obvious instruction. Then it was consuming the souls when they were supposed to be sent to the Underworld and now this—a hostage situation. What the fuck was his goal? Piss off as many gods as possible?

"If Catina's still alive," Elyse murmured, her voice soft and trembling, "maybe he took her to consume her somewhere else."

She sounded defeated, as if her friend were already dead.

I shook my head. "It's not his style. X has been killing in public for a while now. He would've killed her in front of you if he wanted to get to you. That's the bastard thing to do. She's still alive."

"How can you be so sure? What if he changed his mind? What if…?" Elyse glanced at me, her eyes glistening, and my heart melted. She carried defiance in her voice, but her face was pleading. Her gaze begged me to be right.

"Elyse," Poseidon said gently, "Ares is right. X has made a show of his murders all this time. He wouldn't have taken someone to consume her in private. He has an agenda."

She let out a little laugh, and it was a surprise, given the circumstances. "Death has an agenda. How ironic." Hatred fueled her sarcasm.

Apollo sat next to Elyse on her couch and slid his arm around her back. His golden hair spilled over his shoulders, shining like a beacon. Hell, even indoors he was putting on an act of looking divine. Except I wanted to be the one next to her, holding her, making her feel safe. But we were all here for the same reason —to support and help Elyse.

When Apollo called to tell me what happened, I hadn't hesitated. I'd rushed over for Elyse as much as the other guys. And we all had a right to do it. As far as I could tell, we each held a piece of her heart.

Usually, that would've pissed me off. But Elyse cared for each of us differently. And if I could have a love that was unique to me, then she could give Poseidon and Apollo what suited them, too.

Look at me go, such a team player.

Of course, Hades was MIA. No surprise—the guy was hardly available for a chat. He didn't want to be a part of these things. Even though a while ago, the four of us had stood together to be there for Elyse, Hades was still a lone ranger.

I suspected it had something to do with Poseidon being here. The brothers never saw eye to eye. It made me glad I wasn't in contact with my own parents. They didn't exactly love me as much as they did my siblings, so it paid to be a rebel.

"I don't get what he's playing at," Elyse said after sipping her coffee. "What could he possibly want with her?"

"I think he's trying to call you out," Poseidon said.

"But I'm willing to fight him any time," Elyse argued. "What's the point of taking Catina? I was there in the room with him."

"Whatever it is, he's not going to kill her or he'd have done so in front of you," Apollo added, and I agreed with him.

Her brow furrowed. "What's his motivation? What the hell does he want? Was it to taunt me?" Her voice trembled, and her lips pinched together.

I couldn't sit back as she fell apart.

"We'll find her," I said. The other two gods looked at me with a warning, but I meant every word. We'd go out and look for her. There weren't a lot of places X could possibly take her—he was uncomfortable in this world, and if he had an agenda, I had an idea where he might go with the human. But I didn't share that little bit of extra information just yet.

"He's right," Poseidon confirmed. "We'll find her."

Apollo nodded, and I had the strangest sensation we were a team of sorts. I couldn't remember when the gods had last agreed with me, let alone accepted me in their circles. In fact, I couldn't remember it'd happened at all. They tended to hate me for one reason or another. And I accepted that long ago, which was why I did my own thing most of the time.

Usually because I didn't see things the way they did.

But I liked this arrangement. It was something new. It felt good to belong somewhere for a change, and with it came a strange warmth floating through me, heating my skin like rays of a summer sun. And I was more than happy to stand together with these guys if it meant we could help Elyse to bring her friend back.

Catina was just a mortal woman, and she didn't stand a chance against X.

No human did, but I shuddered to think what he was doing to her. X was a fuckhead. I wasn't quite sure how he was a part of Hades, but I would've hated to have an alter ego that was pure darkness. Perhaps that was why Hades was always pissed off.

Still, we'd do what was needed to bring Catina back safe and sound. Not only for the sake of the human woman, but also for Elyse, who deserved to see her friend home without a scratch.

Elyse covered her face, and I knew she was crying again. Somehow, her tears smelled like freshly fallen rain. And it was the saddest damn thing I'd ever experienced.

I yearned to take the pain away.

Looking at the sympathy and helplessness on both Apollo and Poseidon's faces, they felt exactly the same way.

"Hey," Apollo said, gently peeling Elyse's hands away from her face to reveal tear-stained cheeks. "We're going to fix this. There's still hope. He just did this to get to you. And if you keep panicking about it, he's going to win. Don't let him win."

It looked like Apollo's speech had worked a little. Elyse tried to swallow her grief and looked at me. Her dark eyes were bright with tears, and if the situation weren't so dire, I would've thought she was the most beautiful thing in the world.

Scratch that. No matter what she did, she was the most beautiful woman in the universe. Natch.

"Why the hell was X at Catina's?" Elyse asked. "I can't figure out what's going on. Is this Hades?" She posed the last question to Poseidon.

Apollo and I both looked at him, too. But Poseidon shrugged his shoulders. He didn't have an answer either.

"All I know is that he has to be stopped," Poseidon declared.

"Yeah, I've been trying to do that," Elyse snapped. "But I haven't had much luck, have I?"

"Don't forget," I said, interrupting her, "you're not alone in this anymore. You're not supposed to be the only one to save Earth. We're here to help you."

Elyse blinked at me. It was true. Even Poseidon had been sent to rein in Hades, and Apollo had wandered the Earth for the last three centuries, so I wasn't the only guard destined to stand at Elyse's side. Even though I was the only one Zeus had sent to help.

"We'll get her back," Apollo said, reassuring Elyse yet again.

"Yeah," I added. "No matter what, we'll get through this—together."

Apollo and Poseidon both stared at me, their jaws dropped.

Until now, I'd been obtuse, throwing everything they thought about me in their faces. Because if they didn't want to believe I was a hero, I'd show them what a disappointment I could be.

Looking back now, it didn't make sense. Maybe it wasn't such a bad thing to prove them wrong instead.

"What?" I asked when Apollo and Poseidon wouldn't stop gawking.

"Nothing," Apollo said. He pulled Elyse into a hug.

Poseidon sat down on her other side, putting his hand on her knee. I was the only one not in on the action, so I climbed over the coffee table and planted my ass on the wood, facing Elyse with our knees touching. I moved the coffee cup out of the way.

Who said I couldn't be domestic?

My skin prickled with the sensation of...magic?

It seemed when the three of us were together, all of us touching Elyse, the strangest thing happened. Energy flared between us. It tasted a little like my own magic, but also like Elyse's. And Apollo's. And Poseidon's.

Strange.

With the four of us touching, the energy we created grew bigger and stronger, its electricity humming over my flesh. Did the others feel it too?

The invisible current surged between us, growing to such an extent, pulling at each fiber of my being that part of me couldn't help but feel as if we'd be ripped to shreds if we didn't separate ourselves.

Poseidon and Apollo must have felt it too, because they both jumped away from Elyse, breaking contact. I remained the only one still touching her, but I drew long, hard breaths, and her eyes were wide.

"What the hell was that?" She glanced at each of us for an answer, her forehead wrinkling.

I shook my head. None of us seemed to know. But the power had been so intense, almost intoxicating. It left me dizzy, the room spinning around me for a few moments. Imagine if we could use this kind of energy and harness it for something better. It seemed completely volatile right now, but with the four of us together, maybe we could actually beat X.

"Whatever it was, we can't use it as long as we have no idea what to do," Poseidon instructed, his voice deep and authoritative. "What if it's not a new power, but a random effect of our magic?"

Yes, Dad, kill the buzz.

Elyse clenched her jaw. "I don't have time to explore another power right now. I've already been working hard just to master my new ability. And if I'm going to go with you guys to get Catina back, I can't afford to lose control."

"You can't come with us," Apollo said, taking a seat on the sofa's armrest.

Elyse frowned at him. "Yes, I can. She's my friend, and there's no way I'm *not* coming with you."

"We don't even know where we're going," Poseidon argued, standing akimbo.

I watched the two of them go back and forth about

how dangerous it could be since Elyse was ultimately human, even though she had divine abilities.

"She should come," I finally interjected.

Apollo and Poseidon both glared at me.

I lifted my chin. "If she's strong enough to fight X, she's capable of coming with us to get her friend back. Elyse isn't a child. I'm pretty sure she hasn't been for some time now." I smirked at her and winked.

She met my gaze, and her eyes were filled with determination. I slid my glance to her lips and remembered she tasted sweet, like honey. What would the rest of her taste like? Divine, I had no doubt. Yes, I'd go to the ends of the Earth for her. And it was only right she came with us, wherever we had to follow X, Elyse would be part of our team.

She was the type of woman who was dangerous for me to be involved with, because I could fall so desperately in love with her. It would be the end of me if I lost her. And she was human, so loss would be inevitable. But something about her asked me that if I didn't risk being with her, if I didn't give my heart to her, there would be no point in doing everything I did. I needed purpose, otherwise I'd end up wandering forever. Just as I'd done for so many centuries after losing Aphrodite, so either way, I was fucked.

CHAPTER 6

Elyse

*S*ince Catina had disappeared, I'd worked hard so I'd be ready to face X. But I hadn't slept well since she was taken. I prayed every second that she'd be safe, and that Ares was right about X not killing her.

By Friday morning, my muscles ached. I'd pushed as far as my body would allow. Since I'd died the second time, my powers had ramped up to a whole new level, and I was more comfortable in my body now than I had been since Heracles started training me.

But there was still a limit. And I'd reached it today.

I rolled out of bed with a groan and decided to take the day off from training. Working sore muscles was usually the best remedy, but I'd pushed myself so hard lately, a day off wouldn't kill me.

X just hadn't returned. I'd half-expected him to lure me out and fight me, if that was what he'd been trying to do with Catina. If he was taunting me.

At least, that was what everyone else was saying. I wasn't so sure. What if, after everything, Catina turned up dead anyway? My stomach hurt each time I thought about her being tortured, picturing her fear as she faced Death. She didn't deserve this and he'd targeted her only to get to me. X wasn't exactly a merciful guy and sparing her life didn't suit his personality.

A sickness rose through me, but I kept moving, anything to avoid letting myself focus on those horrible thoughts of Catina's captured. I'd begged the gods to tell me where they thought X was hiding, but they had no clue and searched the whole world on my behalf. They reminded me I needed to get ready because X had something planned and would return. They hunted for Catina. So I did my best, tried to hone my skills, but I felt deflated and so lost, unable to concentrate.

But I couldn't think like that. I repeated Apollo's words in my head about not letting X win. But imagining Catina dead was so painful, it left me physically crippled. The last thing I'd ever wanted was for my problems to somehow affect her.

Maybe I was a fool to believe I could continue a human existence while everything else in my world changed.

In the shower, I sat on the tiles warmed by the hot

spray and let the water cascade over my body. I remained in the middle of the cubicle, and the water ran over my face, my nose, my lips. The onslaught on my senses was enough that my mind couldn't over-work. Anything to numb the fear ripping me apart, the grief of what was coming, the guilt of what my connection to Catina had done to her.

I stayed in the shower until the water ran cold. When I climbed out, I toweled off my hair as the sound of the television slowly penetrated my thoughts. At first, I thought nothing of it.

But I hadn't watched television after getting out of bed. It should have been off.

I dressed and crept to the lounge. I expected to find one of my men on my couch. Lately, my apartment had been a halfway house for the gods. I didn't mind—I loved it when I found one of them, or all of them, spread out watching television. Their company brought me a comfort I hadn't experienced since I'd lost my dad. They made my apartment full and cheery and enjoyable.

But this time, when I walked into the living room, the person on my couch was a woman. And I couldn't for the life of me work out who she was or how she'd gotten into my apartment.

She turned her head. She was the most gorgeous woman I'd ever seen. Her pale skin contrasted with her dark hair and deep red lips. Curls cascaded over her shoulders and halfway down her chest. She wore a small crown of intertwined white flowers and green vines. Her eyes were almost black, and her face seemed regal—the face of a deity.

"Elyse," she said with a voice that would give any guy an orgasm. Maybe even a woman because she was stunning. "You're awake."

"What are you doing in my house?" I asked, studying the closed door and shut windows.

She pointed at the television. "We have nothing like this in the Underworld. The best I get is touching one of the souls and watching the life they had."

I frowned. The Underworld?

"Persephone?" In Greek mythology, the only other women in the Underworld were the Fates, and they'd been far from beautiful when Heracles took me into the Underworld to meet with them.

She smiled at me, and her radiating beauty was exquisite. "In the flesh. I've wanted to meet you, you know. Ever since Hades came to Earth, the whole Underworld shivers at the sound of your name."

I sank into the armchair closest to me, unsure why anyone would talk about me in the Underworld. My hair hung in wet strands over my shoulders, soaking the T-shirt I'd pulled on. Was Persephone really in my home?

"You're much prettier than I thought you'd be. You look like your mother," she continued.

I froze on the spot, confused by her reference to my mother, but then again, she was the goddess from the Underworld. "How do you know my mother?" I glanced over at the photo of Mom on the TV stand, figuring Persephone might have seen the picture of us.

"Everyone knows your family, honey, even your mother—married in. The Lowes have a reputation. For fighting evil. For sticking it out and doing your job when everyone else gives up. That's a big deal."

This was crazy. Persephone, Hades's ex, was sitting on my couch having girl chat with me as if it were the most normal thing in the world. I supposed, seeing I was already dating Apollo and Poseidon, and I had a thing for Hades, it shouldn't have been so weird. But hell, it was freaking bizarre.

"Aren't you supposed to be down there?" I asked. "I mean, I don't know how it works now you and Hades are over… Six months, that was the agreement, right?"

She laughed—a gorgeous sound—like chimes in the wind. Mesmerizing, hypnotizing. If *I* gushed so much over a goddess, what impact would she have over humans? Would they fall so deeply in love with her, they'd do anything she requested?

"Everything is on its head now. X running around like a child, doing whatever he wants and not sending the souls to us, is breaking down the Underworld. It's unstable. You'd think the Underworld can't get any worse, but there it is."

I frowned. "So, you're here to tell me I need to fix it? Catch X?"

Persephone leaned closer. "Oh, honey, no one is going to catch X. I'm here because of Hades."

"I don't understand," I replied, but the unease that Hades was to blame surged through my gut.

"I've seen how he looks at you. And I think it's a perfect match. Hades doesn't easily fall in love, you know. Trust me, if anyone knows what Hades is all about, it's me."

My stomach fluttered as I tried to figure out what was going on. "Hades feels nothing for me but a healthy dose of lust."

She laughed again, the tantalizing sounds skipping around me, but I felt as if she knew something I didn't and it irritated me. I shifted in my seat to find a comfortable position.

"Just tell me what's going on," I said.

Persephone sighed. "You're very naïve for someone who's seen so much." Cue the condescension. "Hades has a thing for you."

A thing?

"I don't think so." Between Hades and me, I was the only one who gave a shit about what the other one thought. He didn't even think twice about me after getting off. Which I kept letting him do by sleeping with him because I couldn't resist.

"Honey, I know it's hard to believe," she said. "Trust me, when I first saw the way he looks at you, I thought it was silly, too. But he seems to be serious."

I sighed heavily, ignoring the obvious intrusion of

Persephone spying on Hades and me. None of this made sense. If Hades really had a thing for me, he wouldn't keep kissing and fucking me, then vanishing as if I meant nothing. And so many lives had been lost since he'd arrived.

"What about X?" I asked. "You can't tell me Hades is serious about me and then X keeps killing when he knows what I'm all about."

Persephone shook her head, her dark strands bouncing over her shoulders. "It's not Hades's fault. He can't stop X any more than you can. He decided never to love after me. And I don't blame him. A curse is nothing to scoff at, and it affected both of us severely. But X got out because Hades decided to reject part of himself."

"If he rejected love, why are you saying he has something going on with me?"

Persephone exhaled loudly and crossed one leg over another, reminding me of a school teacher about to educate a student who couldn't work out the assigned homework. "Why don't you make us some coffee? Then we can talk this all through, and I can help you see you're the savior of the world for reasons other than your exceptional fighting skills."

She'd just demanded coffee from me like it was normal. But she was a goddess. And the Queen of the Underworld. Maybe it was normal for her to snap her fingers and everyone jumped. Or didn't, seeing as they were all dead.

I guffawed inwardly at my own joke and stood to put on the kettle.

Persephone followed me to the kitchen. She stood slightly taller than me, her body slim, yet powerful, and she ran her hands over everything, as if she were in a strange place, a tourist in my home.

I guess she was.

When the kettle was on, I leaned my hip against the counter and folded my arms.

"I haven't had a lot of girl time." Persephone hopped onto the counter. She wore a Greek-type robe the color of snow. I'd worn one of those when Apollo took me to Mount Olympus with him in something that had felt like a dream. I'd thought she'd wear something black and dreary, seeing as she lived in the Underworld. "The only conversations I have are with the Fates. Past, Present, Future? It can become a bit of a drag. And they aren't into chitchatting over a cup of coffee." Her smile was still gorgeous.

"I can't even imagine what that must be like," I responded, remembering how much I'd cherished my conversations with Catina, how just the simplest of girl chats eased my tension and helped me gain perspective. Sometimes I got so caught up in my world it was easy to forget another life existed around me. If I had no one to talk to like Persephone did, I'd go mad.

"Oh, honey, you don't want to."

When the kettle boiled, I pulled it off the burner and poured the water into two cups prepped with instant coffee. Part of me wished I had something better to offer the Queen of the Underworld. I handed her a cup and tried not to think too hard about how bizarre this was, about what conversation to start, and to just avoid staring at her in awe. For the last couple of months, I'd been surrounded by gods, but each time I met a new one, I'd ended up captivated by their presence.

Even with Persephone only sitting on my kitchen counter, she held such grace and might as well have been seated on a throne. She carried an air that I could never pull off.

"If Hades can't stop X, what's going on?" I asked, sipping the scalding liquid.

Persephone tried the coffee, her shoulders softening and her mouth curling upward. "By Zeus, this will always be the best thing I've ever tasted. It's not often I get to drink coffee."

I nodded, unsure what to say to that. What did she drink down under? The tears of broken families? I shivered and pushed the morbid thoughts away. I looked at her, waiting for her to answer my question.

"X is upset he's lived in Hades's shadow for so long," she finally explained. "That's funny because there aren't shadows where there's no light. So now he's on a rampage while he can be, consuming souls instead of sending them to Hades's world and maintaining the balance. This is all about destroying Hades."

"Why?" I gripped my cup of coffee. It never once

crossed my mind all this was about killing Hades. Instead, I'd blamed him, when I should have asked more questions and understood the real problem.

Persephone ran a thumb over her lower lip. "Every god received something to rule over. Hades was tricked into the Underworld." I knew about that. "X, or Thanatos, was an unfortunate side effect."

"It's his real Greek name, right?" I asked. "But no one really calls him that here."

Persephone nodded. "It's believed that if you say the name out loud, he'll come to get you before your time is up."

"Well, the ass is proving to be capable of that by cutting innocent victims' time short." Even so, I made a mental note not to say his name again.

Persephone laughed, but I didn't think it was funny.

"The ass," she said softly, the corners of her eyes crinkling from her smile.

"So, what am I supposed to do if I can't stop him?" I asked, unsure why she was even here.

"Allow Hades to get closer to you. He's not a bad person." Persephone's whole demeanor changed, replaced by something serious and godly.

"He's not exactly a good guy, either," I said.

"That's not his fault. He's been forced to rule the Underworld, cursed to marry me, and then, despite it all, we didn't work out. The poor guy keeps losing. But with you, it seems different."

I set my cup down on the counter, my mind swimming with so many thoughts and questions. "I'll never have what it takes to entice someone like Hades," I stated, and I regretted admitting that out loud. Especially to a heavenly deity who could have any man fall at her feet with a single glance. I was the opposite of Persephone in so many ways, and in all honesty, her presence intimidated me. How could I compare to her when it came to drawing a god like Hades to my side?

"Honey, you already did." She placed her cup down and hopped off the counter, touching me on the shoulder. My skin tingled beneath her fingers, the pain in my arm muscles fading away.

Nothing made sense. Hades didn't like me or care about me. He was the bad guy. I'd been trying to convince myself of that all this time, but I'd kept making excuses for him.

"How?" I questioned. "How am I meant to do this?"

"By being yourself. You'll be surprised how much that means to someone who's lived a lie most of his life."

She looked sad when she said those words, her eyes lowering momentarily, her lips pinching slightly. Her voice softened, as if her admission caused her grief. And maybe it had. Hades wasn't the only one affected by the curse. She'd been dragged into the Underworld, her life changed for eternity. How was she meant to find her true love when forced to spend six months of the year in the Underworld?

It seemed as though she was thinking about things,

and I wanted to let her speak. For her to feel free to voice anything. It was what I'd enjoyed most while chatting with Catina. The ability to talk openly. Something we used to do a lot before the gods entered my life.

"I wish I could have loved him how he deserved," Persephone admitted. "By the gods, I tried. I tried so hard, for his sake. Because I was stuck down there, and he loved me so much. But I couldn't do it."

I didn't know how it felt to be forced to love someone, but I imagined what it would be like if I had to pretend that Oliver was mine forever. I cared for him, but it just wouldn't work.

And a couple of centuries could really screw with you.

"What now?" I pulled a packet of chocolate-chip cookies from the pantry. My one treat in the house, and something I'd enjoy with Catina when she'd come over for a girls' night.

My chest hurt as I remembered who Catina was with. I felt guilty for enjoying myself. "Do you know anything about my friend, Catina? X kidnapped her, and maybe… You can sense where X is keeping her." I gripped the cookies, the bag crinkling in my hands.

She stared at me for a long time as if processing the question, then raised her palms up and out. "Honey, I wish I could help, but he's connected with Hades, and I haven't felt him around for weeks now. I'm sorry I can't help more."

My stomach sank, but I held on to the hope we'd find her.

"To sort out this huge mess, you need to start realizing Hades isn't the bad guy and give him a chance. It might be the answer you're seeking," Persephone said. She swallowed a mouthful of coffee, but her eyes stayed on me. And I had no reason to believe she had an ulterior reason for visiting. She sounded genuine, and maybe she knew more about X than she led on.

"So, me being with Hades will help keep X under control?" I asked, stating the point Persephone seemed to avoid directly saying.

A blank expression fell over her face. "Difficult to know the exact reason X broke free, but Hades needs to learn to love again, so it's worth trying."

So I'd try to listen to her advice, which was much easier said than done. You didn't just decide a bad guy was a good guy because someone else said so. But I'd wanted to trust Hades from day one. And maybe now I'd be able to.

After he proved himself, of course.

Because I was a lot of things, but naïve wasn't one of them, regardless of what Persephone believed.

CHAPTER 7

Apollo

*E*lyse had changed since the last time she died. She was a lot stronger, yes, but it was more than sheer physical strength. She'd been so angry before, so unsure about who she was going to become. But she was different now—sure of herself, settled in her power, and looking forward instead of back. Even after the shit X had pulled, I had to admit I admired everything about her, from her confidence in the face of such a horrific time to her tenderness—caring so much for her friend, insisting she'd search every corner of the planet to find X and save her.

We spent all of Saturday together, spending time in each other's company.

Comforting her, I insisted on going out for a walk with her for fresh air. Lake Michigan was spectacular, and there were a few people around, but it was quiet as we strolled side by side next to the water.

I listened to her talk, and I was fascinated by her human life—an existence she seemed more and more uncomfortable with. With each passing day since I first met her, she seemed less human to me. No matter how much she insisted she wasn't a deity.

Catina was Elyse's link to her humanity, and she held on to that connection for dear life. I'd figured that out pretty soon after meeting the girl. Now with Catina taken, I tried to do whatever it took to distract Elyse until we found X, to stop her from falling apart because her tears broke me. Yet I kept wondering if she felt like it was symbolic, that her humanity was fading and Catina had disappeared, too.

Though again, I hoped she didn't feel that way. Her compassion, her emotional strength, her will to lay down her lives—all four of them—for others, was her human side showing through.

The gods could be pretty damn selfish. Ironic, if you considered how much life we had to live. But we took our immortality for granted and too often gave little thought to the grief humans went through. Sure, we observed them, but for us, the souls went on to another realm, so life never truly ended.

"Talk to me," I murmured softly, taking her hand in mine, our fingers intertwined. She felt tiny in my palm, and more than anything, I wanted to fold her into my arms and keep her guarded from X, from grief, from agony. But she'd never accept that. She'd been brought up a warrior who fought against danger, not a victim who ran away. So, I'd remain by her side as I had done since we first met, there for her when she needed me.

"I don't want to talk about Catina if that's what you mean," she finally replied, glancing up at me, her eyes glazed. They were still red from her earlier crying, her cheeks rosy and so flawless like the rest of her.

My chest tightened. I didn't mind what she talked about to me as long as she didn't shut me out. "We can chat about anything."

"Persephone came to see me," she said softly.

"What?" I looked at her, frowning. We'd spent the whole day together, and she hadn't mentioned that piece of information.

Elyse kept staring at me without answering. She knew I'd heard her.

"She's not supposed to be able to come to Earth yet," I explained.

"That's what I thought, too. But apparently, the Underworld is unstable because of what X is doing. It's falling apart."

I tried to piece together what Elyse was saying. X's actions had repercussions far worse than I'd imagined. If the Underworld was unsteady, what would that mean for the dead souls? The fates? To the balance for humans? Zeus ruled over the domains with his two brothers to maintain perfect harmony, but if one element stopped working, everything would soon start breaking down.

"She said it's not Hades." Elyse's voice sliced through my thoughts. "Apparently, X is acting on his own. Because Hades is in such a bad place X was able to escape."

"That doesn't make sense," I said. "Hades and X are supposed to be stuck to each other. X is his alter ego."

Elyse glanced around as if looking for answers. "To be honest, I don't know enough about X to tell you if you're right or wrong. I never learned about him in school or from my dad. He's not a popular topic in Greek mythology. Which is why he's pissed off, it seems. Or something like that. Persephone said Hades needs to learn to love again, and I must give him a chance. What am I supposed to do with that?"

I ran my hands through my hair. What the hell had just happened? We hadn't talked about anything important the whole day, and now she'd blurted out a vital piece of information?

"Okay," I acknowledged.

"Okay?" She looked at me, her brow furrowed.

"Yeah. Thanks for telling me."

Elyse shrugged again, and we continued walking. "Just thought this might mean something to you. Clearly not," she said, her voice darkening.

But my mind was racing, far away, with Hades. I drew her into my arms and wrapped them around her. My heart beat erratically in my chest whenever I held her, when our bodies pressed close, and I wanted nothing more than to keep her safe for eternity.

The breeze fluttered through her long, chestnut hair, a striking contrast to her pale skin. All I could remember was her smile when I'd whisked her off to ride in my chariot, how I'd promised myself to do whatever it took to give her endless joy and wipe away the grief.

"I'm going to find out what it means." I brushed a strand of hair off her cheek.

Her mocha eyes carried a softness to them, and she melted against my chest, her arms looping around me. With her cheek just over my heart, I touched my chin on the top of her head and knew exactly who'd help find the answer we sought.

*P*oseidon

Later that day, I appeared in front of Hades's dump. Apollo came to tell me what Elyse had said to him and thought I'd do a better job of getting more information out of my brother. I wasn't sure it would work, but Hades would more likely speak to me than Apollo.

If my brother wasn't at fault here, why didn't he help us stop X? I couldn't stand that my brother hurt as much as he did. First Persephone, and now X's atrocities on his conscience? If it was true, of course.

"What do you want?" Hades blurted when he opened the door.

"We have to talk," I said.

He rolled his eyes but he let me in. "I don't really want company."

"Too bad," I grumbled. "What's going on with you and X?"

Hades groaned. "Why does everyone think I'm the one to blame for this?"

"Because it's X, Hades," I said. "Because he's always been a part of you. But Persephone doesn't seem to think so."

Hades's frustration morphed into a glare almost immediately. "You talked to her?" he snarled. "What the fuck made you think it's okay to chat with my ex? God, nothing is sacred with you people, is it?"

"Calm down. She's my family too, so of course I'll talk to her if I need to." Fuck, his irritation was getting to me because I felt jumpy, as if I wore a straitjacket and just needed to break free. "But this time, I didn't talk to her. She came to Earth and looked up Elyse."

Hades blinked at me, as shocked about the news as I'd been.

"You're kidding me, right? You're just here to fuck with me."

I sighed and walked to one of the couches facing the television. The inside of the house was fit for a king, with lush furnishing, paintings on the pearl white walls, and exquisite rugs. It was just the outside that resembled a crap-heap. But I understood what Hades was trying to do. I glanced around, and I wondered if it was the case with him as a person, too. Was he a dick on the outside but nice on the inside? Did that mean Persephone's message was real because she truly cared for him?

There was no way I'd know if his good side was real. He was so damn shut off from the rest of us. Had always been that way.

"Trust me," I finally said. "I wouldn't go out of my way only to fuck with you. I'm serious. Elyse is a little unsure about what to make of the visit."

"Well, she should just reject anything that witch said about me."

I pushed my shoulders back. "She said you're not to blame for what X is doing."

That pulled Hades up short. He flopped down in an armchair, his legs planted wide, his elbows on his knees. His face was incredulous.

"She said that?" he asked in a softer voice, his gazed fixed on the rug under his feet.

"Yeah. She's coming to your defense, believe it or not."

"Why the fuck would she do that?" he questioned.

It was a damn shame he was so used to being treated badly that he couldn't fathom someone wouldn't want to hurt him.

"Look, I'm sorry about all of this." The words were

hard to say, but what if I'd been wrong this whole time, blaming my brother unjustly?

Hades narrowed his eyes at me. "What do you mean, you're sorry?"

"How many meanings can an apology have?" I asked. "Seriously, I thought you were a dick, looking for attention. I was wrong. I didn't realize that this thing with you and Persephone was so serious."

"Did you think we were playing happy family for centuries to humor Hera after she cursed me?" Hades sneered, straightening his posture.

I sighed. He was so angry, but who could blame him?

"That's the point I'm making," I said carefully replied, articulating each word. "I realize now how hard the breakup had to be. I want to be here for you now because I wasn't before."

Hades let out a sarcastic laugh and reclined in the seat. "Well, aren't you just so noble? The hero brother looking out for the mistake."

"You know that's not what this is," I snapped, reeling in the fire burning in my chest. Hades always pushed my buttons.

He slapped his thighs and stood up. "Whatever you need to tell yourself, asshole. Don't act like you give a shit about how I feel now. If you cared that much, you would've stopped Hera from playing her games when she cursed me to fall in love with Persephone. And you wouldn't have exiled me to the Underworld."

"Are we still on this?" I started, but he went on.

"Don't come to my house, intrude on my time, and sit your self-righteous ass on my couch to pretend like you fucking care, Poseidon. You've never given a shit. You had a hell of a long time to fix this, and to be frank, it's far too little, too fucking late."

I stood, also, the rage pouring through me. "Do you think you're the only one who suffers?"

"What have you gone through, Oh Mighty God of the Seas? What have you struggled with that makes us the same?"

"I have to stand between you and Zeus all the time. Do you know how often I have to give up my own life to sort out some shit between the two of you?"

"Spare me, Poseidon," he growled, rolling his eyes. "Don't act like that's half as bad as what you did to me. Besides, if you guys hadn't fucked me over, there wouldn't have been fights to mediate, so I think you got what was coming to you."

I groaned. This was never going to go anywhere. We always revolved around to the same problem, over and over. He'd never forgive Zeus and me.

"Why don't you get over it?" I barked. "It happened at the beginning of time! That's a long while to hold a grudge."

"Why don't you just fuck off and leave me alone?" Hades marched out of the room and down a corridor, vanishing into the house.

I didn't have to do what he said, but the conversation was over unless I followed him. And I wasn't a sucker for pain. This was unnecessary. He wasn't going to tell me anything about Persephone or X, not in his shitty mood.

I'd come here to reach out to Hades, not to fight.

So, I "fucked off" as he'd said. I left his shitty house and stormed down the road, seething. The clouds overhead crowded together, and hard raindrops fell around me. Not on me, but the world surrounding me was soon drenched, rivets of water running under my boots, splashing with each footfall.

Did I feel like shit about what Zeus and I had done to Hades? Yes. Did I hate that it practically ruined the relationship between my brother and me? Absolutely.

Was Hades going to forgive me? Probably not.

But I was sorry that I'd put him through so much, and for years I'd tried to mend the bridge between Hades and me, but I could never do enough. I saw that now.

I could only try for so long. Maybe the damage was so deeply entrenched in our history that there was no coming back, simply no way to mend our relationship.

I'd always assumed we'd one day get over the past one day, but now I wasn't sure. It had taken me too long to understand how deeply this affected Hades. And now in my heart, I retracted all the bad things I'd ever said and done to him.

Guilt clawed at me. I'd hurt him and it was unfair that he'd wound up in an even worse spot than before.

With Persephone leaving him, he'd probably realized he was hard to love. And more than anything, I wanted to be there for him and help him. But I couldn't change what happened in the past. I wished Hades could understand that. Whatever ensued back then was in the past and no matter what happened from now on, the only direction to move was forward. I had to somehow make Hades open his eyes.

For a moment, I considered talking to Zeus. This was as much his problem as it was mine, after all. But I decided against it. Zeus wasn't involved in all this bull-shit on Earth thanks to X being set free. And Zeus had already taken care of what he could by appointing the Lowe family to protect the humans from godly monsters. Knowing him, he'd just as likely banish us from humans altogether, leaving them to their own devices. And as selfish as it sounded, I didn't plan to lose Elyse.

But the three of us—Zeus, Hades, and me—couldn't fight until the end of time.

At some point, I had to take responsibility for what had happened between us, without Zeus.

It was a strange concept, but I couldn't only be the mediator like I always was. It might be a bitter pill to swallow, but I'd been a dick, too.

CHAPTER 8

Elyse

The only way to deal with everything going wrong in my life was to work out. Training wasn't only my day job these days, it was also my escape. I pushed myself so hard that thinking about my problems was out of the question.

And I had a hell of a lot to escape from.

Since X took Catina, there'd been no sign of her. I didn't know where he was keeping her, and it ate me up inside each time I thought about what she'd be going through. Was she still alive? I'd searched all over Chicago, looking everywhere I could think of, and anywhere that was darker than it should have been. Old buildings, rundown joints, and even the underground tunnels.

I wiped my cheeks of tears.

I'd asked Poseidon to call an audience with Zeus to help us out, but he insisted calling him might not necessarily result in the answer we wanted. He wouldn't say anymore, so I left it. Some things were better left unsaid when it came to Zeus. If Heracles said Zeus's help came with more complications, I believed it.

X was connected to Hades, and only Hades had power over him, not Zeus. A situation the king of Mount Olympus had created when he segmented the Earth and straight divided it between him and his brothers. So it came back to Hades. Always him. Which the other gods were on top of, they insisted. They were running around to find Catina and telling me to stay safe and keep training. But it killed me to sit back. Especially when all of us had no clue where X was hiding.

A sickness sat permanently in my chest, and I could barely eat since my thoughts were with my friend every second of the day.

Catina's job was on the line as Tina had called me looking for her, threatening to fire her if she didn't appear. And while that wasn't as high a priority as her life, Catina would be devastated to lose the job she adored and had worked so hard to keep. For that reason, I opened a missing persons file at the police station. Tina couldn't fire her if this wasn't Catina's fault. So, she'd at least have a job once she returned. *Please let her come back in one piece.*

Of course, the police wouldn't find her. Even if they put their best detectives on the job. But they wouldn't do that, anyway. Too many people were nowhere to be found in Chicago, too many other crimes took precedence. She was just another missing persons case.

It only pissed me off more, even though I'd knew this would be the outcome. What about the families out there who had no hope but to rely on the cops for their absent loved ones? On the bright side, Catina's parents were alive, so the cops could contact them to ask questions about her disappearance.

I was beating the living shit out of a punching bag at the training center. I hadn't wrapped my hands; I'd barely warmed up, but so much pent-up anger and stress and sorrow burrowed inside me. And I had no idea how else to deal with the fiery anger burning me up. Grief surged with every exhale, and nothing I did soothed the agony and regret over the fact that I should have kept my distance from Catina. Then X wouldn't have targeted her. The emptiness in my heart left me hollow, and numbness thundered in my head. Tears crammed in the corners of my eyes, and I wiped the moisture with a shoulder. But I kept hitting the bag. Harder. Faster. Until it hurt so much I felt nothing else.

"Are you trying to kill it?" Ares asked behind me. I stared at him in the full-length mirror behind the punching bag. He wore jeans and a muscle tee. It seemed that look was his thing. He also had a pair of wraparound sunglasses on his head that looked silly with his hair cropped so short. Ares had never fit in, yet it worked on him perfectly.

I ignored him and kept hitting. He couldn't make this pain go away, so I'd do it myself.

"Elyse," he said. "Stop."

No fucking way. I slammed the bag harder and harder.

"Elyse." Ares's voice climbed, and suddenly he stood next to me. He grabbed my wrists to stop me from striking and held them so we could both see my hands. My knuckles were raw and there were smears of blood smudged across the bag.

"Fight me instead," Ares insisted.

I frowned. "I'll get blood on your shirt."

"Yeah, I don't care about that. Seriously. Fight me. It will help."

I avoided eye contact with him. "I'm not going to hit you, Ares. I just need to blow off some steam."

"And combat is how you do it. I get it. Trust me, if there's anyone who gets it, it's me. It helps when you're battling some*one*. That poor bag doesn't stand a chance, and you won't feel better, anyway."

I narrowed my eyes at him. Why was he so nice? Then I remembered our kiss, and how incredible he felt, how he made me forget myself.

"I'm not here to look for trouble," he said in a soft voice, as if he'd heard my thoughts. "You should know that by now."

I was starting to know Ares a little better, and he was

85

nothing like what I'd first thought. Of course, I still remained wary of him, but that worry was born from stories I'd heard from others, and from what the history books said about him. I was realizing they were all wrong.

"Fine," I agreed. "But you're not dressed for it."

Ares pulled down his jeans.

"Jesus," I said when he stood in front of me with just his jock strap on, his package as clear as day. Were my cheeks burning up?

"Better?" He winked.

I laughed despite myself. "If you win, it'll be cheating. No distractions."

"You won't have time to stare," Ares teased, and his fist shot out at me before the vibrations in the air carrying his words even stopped shaking.

I ducked, moving faster than I'd been able to before. I was getting used to my new strength, my speed, the power that flowed through my veins.

I retaliated, threw fist after fist, and kicked. We fell into a rhythm. It wasn't a fight, it was more like aggressive sparring. And it could do enough damage if we hadn't both known what we were doing.

But Ares was ready for me every step of the way. And he'd been right. It helped to let out the frustration, the bubbling energy, the grief. We fought for an hour straight. Maybe more.

When I threw a punch and as he ducked, my body followed the momentum. He swung around and looped an arm across my stomach, catching me and keeping me from falling over.

"Thank you," I whispered, breathing hard, and we both collapsed on the floor, gasping for air.

But he was barely breaking a sweat. The gods really had all the good and none of the bad.

"Don't mention it. Feel like talking about what's going on now?"

I groaned. "The point of this sparring was so I don't have to think about what's bothering me."

"Humor me," he said. "I promise it will help. And I was right the first time, wasn't I?"

I couldn't argue with him, especially when he sat next to me not wearing much, and I kept fighting the urge to lower my gaze.

"I feel helpless," I admitted. "I wasn't able to save Catina. X took her because of me."

"X caught you off-guard," Ares said.

"But that's just it. When does he ever warn us he's going to kill someone? That he took Catina is just proof I suck at my job. I'm all tied up about her disappearing when I haven't been nearly this upset about every other soul X consumed. I'm supposed to look after humans, but what have I been doing?"

"What you can," Ares responded, putting his hand on mine, his skin heated.

I lay on the floor and he did the same alongside me. I turned my head toward him. His eyes were like emeralds and so intense I felt as if he were staring right into my soul.

"It's not enough," I said. "All those innocents have families who are grieving for them, and I should have done more to help."

"So," Ares replied, rising up on his elbow next to me, "do more."

It sounded so simple when he said it. And maybe it was, but the thought of doing *even more* never hit me this hard before. Catina's kidnapping had messed me up, and I couldn't find a way to stop the sorrow from shackling me.

"Do you ever lose?" I asked to change the topic. "When you fight?"

"I lost against you."

I could see the flecks of silver in his eyes.

His angular jaw, distinct cheekbones, and tanned skin made him devilishly handsome.

I raised my eyebrows. "Sparring doesn't count."

"I wasn't talking about training." His voice was rugged and so sexy.

His eyes bored into me even deeper, and I realized what he was saying. He felt something for me beyond physical attraction. And if I had to be honest with myself, which I was trying to be these days, my feelings were growing for him, too.

And this time, there was no guilt that I was wrong about my attraction. Because underneath all that bravado and aggression, Ares was really a nice guy.

And way too similar to me in ways that made me want to spend hours with him chatting about training and the universe—and one day, I'd be curious to know what the heck his deal was with Aphrodite. Only out of curiosity, in fact, not jealousy.

The atmosphere shifted around us, and my power flared, tingling over my flesh, bubbling in my chest like an inferno. A scorching heat surrounded us, pressing against me as if I wore a fur coat. When I met Ares's gaze, his face was so close I could breathe him in. His nose tickled mine.

I let out a tiny gasp but didn't move away. A light crackling sounded in the air as it had last time we'd come together, the excitement of having the God of War all to myself.

His hand moved to my hip as we lay on the training mats, his lips softly grazing mine. We'd done this before, kissing after fighting.

Now, I craved him like a drug, needing the escape he offered. His tongue slipped into my mouth, and I moaned. I thought about wrapping my arm around his neck, but I didn't know if that was cliché. Ares was so different from the other gods.

Albeit just as attractive.

The kiss changed. He'd been tentative when he started. Now, he kissed me hungrily, sucking my lip into his mouth, his hand pushing under the loose shirt I wore. His touch trailed fire on my skin, and my body adopted the heat, warmth flushing through me.

One inhale of his musky scent turned me on. I loved the way he kissed me. Like nothing mattered. Like we could fix the world. Like only I existed in his life. I'd come here for an escape, and if this was what freedom looked like, I was going to take it.

Ares pushed my shirt up and broke the kiss, studying me as he revealed my skin inch by inch. I lifted my torso, and he pulled the shirt over my head.

"I hate sports bras," he announced.

I chuckled. When Ares shifted again, I noticed his dick in his jock strap. He stood rock hard and ready for me. I breathed deep. In and out. Time was forgotten. Everything was in that moment. My clothes were a hindrance, and I needed them off.

I shivered. I desired him. I craved all of him.

If he wanted the sports bra gone, I'd get rid of the garment. It wasn't easy to take off, not for someone else, so I wriggled out of it. Ares's eyes rested on my breasts, and I stared him right in the face. I was far from an insecure girl who wanted to cover up. Power rippled through me, and even though I wasn't a goddess, I was damn close to feeling like one.

I saw Ares as an equal, and in his presence, he never made me feel anything less.

He kissed me again, rougher, the stubble on his chin chafing my skin. His hands roamed my body, tweaking my nipples, tugging at my skintight workout pants.

"We're not going to be alone for much longer," I

said, breaking the kiss. "The training center is actually for other people, too."

"Fuck 'em."

I laughed. "Yeah, but I'd prefer not to put on a show."

He stood, pulling me up. He lifted me with ease, and I wrapped my legs around his waist. I kissed him while he walked me across the training hall to a side office. When he tried the handle, it was locked. I squirmed, wanting him to let me down. He planted me on the floor next to him.

"We can't go in there," I said.

Ares kicked the door, and it splintered at the lock, swinging open.

"That's destruction of property," I pointed out as I swept kisses across his cheek and neck. Hell, he smelled and tasted like candy on a stick.

"They can bill me." Ares dragged me into the office. He shut us inside and hauled the desk so it held the door in place. I giggled. This was a different side of him. Urgent, serious. But sensual.

I loved it.

When he turned, he was on me again. I worked my way up his chiseled body, noting how different he was from the other gods I'd been with. Lean muscle. He wasn't as heavy built as Apollo or as tall as Poseidon, but he was a war machine, and every muscle that rippled under his skin was for fighting, not for show.

Ares tugged my pants down. I stood naked, while he

kicked off his jock strap. There was little ceremony to what we were doing, no foreplay as such. But we didn't need it. I'd been turned on by him from our last kiss, from the lingering arousal between us. Plus, fighting him drew me closer to him.

I was turned on as hell, my whole body buzzing, the heat between my legs so wet. Yep, I eagerly craved release. And I got the feeling that Ares was always straight to the point when it came to this.

He sat me on the desk, and I opened my legs. His cock was hard and bobbed when he stepped closer. He kissed me at the same time as his fingers found my clit, and I gasped into his mouth.

He only flicked his fingers over my clit for a short while, enough to make me beg for more, before pushing me back. I lay on the table while files folders dug into my spine, but I didn't care.

When he positioned himself between my legs, I was more than ready for him. His cock speared into my wetness, and I groaned.

Immediately, Ares started fucking me with quick caresses that were as deep as they were urgent. He kissed me, his tongue probing my mouth for a moment before he lifted his head. He balanced on his arms, his legs wide between mine, splaying me open. I let out a moan as he stroked my pussy, relieving an ache I hadn't known I felt.

He fucked me harder and faster, and my moans turned into cries. He bucked his hips against me, and the burning friction intensified. A fire might as well have been alight within me as I built toward a first orgasm. And it roared through me.

When I came, Ares pressed his mouth against mine to swallow my screams of pleasure, grunting when my insides clamped down on him.

I barely recovered before he started again. It wasn't the kind of fuck that you just got off on. Every bit of this was connected and close, sensual, even though it was rough. I had the feeling this was just how Ares was. He didn't do slow and careful.

And that was fine by me. I didn't need slow and careful, not from him. Not now with my life being a shitstorm. I don't know how long we rocked, but it felt like hours.

I orgasmed again. It was impossible to hold back with his onslaught and the way he made me feel. Ares didn't kiss me this time. Instead, he threw his head back and growled like an animal, before his cock kicked inside me as he came, too. His lips probed mine, and he kissed me long and hard, and I loved falling under his attention, never wanting to come up for air.

But when we finally pulled apart, the atmosphere grew hot and sticky between us, my body a lot number than I'd ever been from training. We'd been in the office for almost an hour.

"We have to get out of here." I pulled myself up, and yanked on my underwear and holding my pants, stared toward the exit.

The sounds of people training on the other side of the office door filtered in. I wondered how much they'd heard.

"You don't have a top or bra on," Ares pointed out, eyeing me while smirking.

Shit. I'd left them in the training hall.

"Wait here," Ares said as he opened the door, pushing the desk out of the way as if it weighed nothing. I hopped off and pulled on my pants, letting the material soak up the aftermath of our sex without cleaning up. I'd shower at home. Right now I was freaking out about how someone could have busted in on us having sex. My worry was more that kids were out there.

Ares returned a little while later with my bra, my top, and my duffel bag.

"Some of the students looked at me funny," he said with a grin.

I laughed and pulled the clothes on, grateful to be able to cover up. When I was dressed, Ares kissed me.

"Let's go," he stated. He pulled me against him, and we left the office so fast, I hardly saw who was in the hall. Somehow, we weren't spotted by the people training. Maybe they were too busy with their burpees to notice us leaving from the office with the busted lock.

Or he'd done something to cloak us somehow.

Either way, he was a hell of a lot of fun, and I definitely wanted more.

CHAPTER 9

Hades

This was some ridiculous bullshit. *Sometimes you just can't win, right?* In my case, I never won. I'd somehow drawn the short straw when it came to life in general. Shit kept snowballing my way no matter what I did.

And considering I was immortal, "life" was a fucking long thing to trudge through. All those years when I thought I'd found the real thing with Persephone, I embraced my role in the Underworld, loved waking up next to her every day for half the year, and believed I'd found the secret to happiness. What a fucking load of crap. I'd fallen under a curse and been a laughing stock, and now the burning anger rose through me like a volcano ready to explode.

Plus, I was pissed off about Poseidon's visit. He came to tell me Persephone was here. What the hell was she doing on Earth? It was my turf now. She wasn't welcome. I'd left the Underworld so we didn't have to stare at each other every day when we obviously didn't fit together anymore.

Anymore? Try never. The whole fucking relationship had been a joke, anyway. A curse from my bitch of a sister, with Persephone trying her best to do something she just didn't believe in because I'd trapped her into spending eternity with me.

How fucking romantic.

I was so over this shit. I was over the stupid breakup, and I sure as hell wasn't ready for any sympathy. Especially not from my brother. Because he wasn't sympathetic toward me, he was just nosy. He wanted to know what Persephone was doing here, too. And he had to know if I knew.

It wasn't hard to find her. Centuries together meant I recognized her power signature better than I knew my own. It was just a case of tuning into the right vibes and following it until I found her. Her energy flowed like silk over my flesh, and I grabbed that connection and trailed it, vanishing from my home and tracing Persephone's power source to a hotel.

She stayed in the Ritz-Carlton, as if she were some kind of royalty. She'd probably charmed herself into a free suite.

"What are you playing at?" I demanded, materializing into her room. "Do you think this is funny?"

"Hades," Persephone said with a sigh, standing near the grand window but turning away from the picturesque view of the city below. "I thought I'd see you sooner or later."

"Damn straight you're going to have to answer to me. What the fuck do you think you're doing looking up people in my life?"

"You don't have some kind of monopoly when it comes to Earth." She gripped her hips, reminding me of all our past arguments where she'd dug her heels in, and glared at me like she was preparing to send an army of the dead to hunt me down. As if she could.

"And it's a pity because I'd get rid of scum like you," I sneered, hating that I let my anger take control. But I couldn't stop the fury raging inside me.

An expression of exhaustion danced across on her features. I'd once considered her adorable with her petite nose and plump lips, but now they just reminded me of my humiliation. Of how I'd been played.

She drew in a sharp breath, releasing it before speaking. "I'm not here to fight with you, Hades."

"Well, I'm here to fight with you," I said, cutting off whatever else she was going to say. "You involve yourself in business that has nothing to do with you."

She returned her attention to the window and looked out over Chicago, a place I'd called home for the last couple of months. It wasn't her world. She could go right back where she'd came from.

As she stood with her back to me, I studied her like someone else would. I tried to see her as a person I hadn't been cursed to love once upon a time.

She looked lovely, there was no doubt about that, with a gorgeous body. And she was a nice person on top of that. She worked hard for a long time to give me what I'd looked for in our relationship. She could have hated me, pushed me away, but instead she endeavored to make it work. But a person could only pretend for so long, and even though she'd done the right thing— she had tried, she'd given me everything when I'd tricked her into staying in the Underworld with me— all I saw when I looked at her was resentment.

"So, are you just going to stand there?" I asked when she stared out at the city without saying a word. It was as if she expected me to ogle her. And I was furious that I'd fallen for it.

"The Underworld is unraveling," she said, turning around.

I frowned at her comment, at the concern in her voice. It was hard to think such a shitty, dark place could get any worse.

"It's why I've come," she added. "Things are obviously not going very well up here, so I thought I'd do what I can to help."

"Ha!" I barked. "You have no idea what's going on."

Persephone lifted her chin. "I know a lot more than

you think. I'm aware you're hurt about what happened with us, that you're mad at Hera, and somehow you think taking it out on me will help."

"Don't even go there," I warned. "I'm not in the mood for games."

"And I'm not playing any," she said tightly, her lips pinching.

"Look, I don't want you here. I don't want anything to do with you. I know it's not your fault, but I don't have to face you if I don't want to. It's the reason I left you alone down there, for fuck's sake! Something had to give."

She drew in a sharp breath and strolled past me, the fabric of her white dress sashaying around her legs. She swung her hips from side to side, and her long hair brushed her perfect ass. But I wasn't turned on by her anymore. It was funny how a broken heart could translate into a limp dick.

"Was it Poseidon?" Persephone asked.

I narrowed my eyes at her. "How would you know who came to talk to me? Have you been watching me?"

"I'm just trying to make sure you're okay. But I didn't spy on you. He's just the most likely to try and fix things. He feels so terrible about what happened between you, him, and Zeus." Her voice sounded genuine, and her tone held no hint of mockery or sarcasm, but I didn't need to deal with her overprotectiveness right now when I felt like shit.

I turned my back on her. I wasn't even going to

listen to that crap anymore. Everyone always advocated for my brothers, saying they were so fucking great. Well, I knew otherwise.

Was I holding a grudge? You bet. But you didn't get your entire life—which was an eternity—ruined and not feel something. It hurt like a bitch, and I wasn't going to forgive and forget like everyone was expecting me to.

When things went well with Persephone, I wasn't so pissed off, except for when she'd leave to spend six months of summer in the upper world. Then I thought about letting it all go. But that had failed and all the hell that had gone wrong in my life smacked me in the face, and the smile and wave routine exhausted me when I seethed on the inside.

"I'm out of here," I said, marching toward the door, as if I needed to use it to walk away from her. I could just poof out of the hotel, and she wouldn't be able to do a thing about it. But part of me wanted her to call me back and say something. I didn't know what I was waiting for. An apology was unfair because this wasn't her fault any more than it was mine. I was a fucking contradiction.

But I was sick and tired of everyone else being so damn accepting of their fate.

"Oh," I clipped, turning around and snapping at her when she wasn't the one to call me back. "Don't talk to Elyse again, either."

"What?" Persephone challenged. "You don't have the right to tell me whom I can and can't see."

"No, but I can tell you to stay the fuck out of my business and talking to Elyse falls in that category. It's. My. Business. So leave her alone."

Persephone crossed her arms in front of her chest. "I wish you'd just accept you're in love with her."

Her words were a punch to the gut. She didn't hold back and was always so blunt.

"I don't do love, Persephone. Don't you remember?" Thank fuck that gods didn't blush, because I'd have been in trouble. "It's why Hera cursed me in the first place—so that even the awful God of the Underworld could fall in love. It took a curse to do that. And no one has been throwing curses around lately for me to fall into the same trap twice."

She stared at me intensely with a lecturing gaze. "You're not unlovable, you know."

"You didn't want me," I responded bitterly and too fast.

"Because we weren't meant to be together," she argued, her voice climbing slightly. "Didn't you ever ask the Fates?"

I rolled my eyes. Persephone loved asking them about her future, as if it would change from the previous week, when she'd last asked. When you didn't die, everything else became a pebble in a river that kept on flowing. Eventually, time sanded it down until it didn't matter anymore.

So, knowing all the good and all the bad that would happen to us had become a pastime for Persephone. A hobby, her obsession.

"I don't ask them about things I don't care about." I huffed and watched her stroll over to the edge of the king-sized bed and sit on the end.

"Or things you do," she said softly. "But I bet you wondered about Elyse. Didn't you? I see how you look at her."

I was about ready to blow my lid. "Can't you find something better to do with your time?" I snapped.

"Not since you trapped me down there. It's a bore, and I need something to occupy myself with."

She was just as quick as I was. I could've fallen for someone who wasn't half as sharp. But it'd been Persephone, and I'd been doomed to arguments that were never resolved because neither of us could admit to being wrong.

"All I'm saying is stay away from her," I fumed tightly.

"And I'm saying allow yourself to feel."

I released an impatient snort. That was the one thing I wouldn't do because it came with regret, humiliation, and pain.

"You know what?" she said, and I hated the sarcastic tone of her voice. It sounded as though she was done arguing and that always made me feel like I'd lost the fight. "It's fine. You just carry on doing you without noticing everyone who reaches out to you."

"Who reaches out to me?" I asked.

Persephone closed her eyes as if her head hurt. But it was something she'd seen humans do. Gods and goddesses didn't get headaches. She had a habit of trying out human mannerisms after watching what they did up on Earth, like the time she went through a 'totally' phase, using the word in front of every sentence, until I banned anyone from using it in the Underworld because it drove me insane.

"You're never going to change," she began, opening her eyes again and meeting my gaze. "It's a pity, because she has so much to offer."

I didn't want to hear any more. I was tired of being told I was the one in the wrong when everyone else messed with me. I was tired of being forgotten when all I wanted was to be loved.

Which was pretty damn pathetic, anyway.

So, I disappeared from Persephone's room, leaving behind the woman I'd once loved.

I visualized myself vanishing, and the world around me evaporated. In a split second, I took form again in my house on the bad side of town. Just as I collapsed on my bed, X appeared in the corner, black fog swirling around his feet, his eyes filled with eternal fire as he grinned.

"I'm not in the mood for your shit," I said, deliberately looking away. Why the fuck didn't anyone leave me alone?

"But you can't get rid of me. It's not really up to you if I stay or go."

I groaned. Somehow, he'd escaped my control, and I ought to have been angry, but I was exhausted and frustrated. I wasn't sure what the hell he wanted from me.

"Why the fuck can't you leave the humans alone?" I demanded to know.

He hovered there like a nightmare. "You have no power over me."

It looked like it was my fault, but it wasn't. I wished it was so I could do something about him, fix up this mess of him targeting innocents. But it was out of my hands, and I already had so much to deal with, I didn't know what do to anymore.

I covered my face with my hands and wished it would actually help.

Elyse flashed before me. Her dark hair, her big eyes, the way she looked at me when I felt like the rest of the world fell away.

Persephone was right. Of course she was. She knew me well enough to always be right about me. I was in love with Elyse. But I wasn't going to admit it to anyone.

I looked up and X was gone. Thank fuck.

Being in love only brought me pain before. And Persephone remained in my life, showing up where she wasn't wanted.

If that was what happened when I loved, I wasn't

going to go for that shit again. Love was grand and all, but it hurt too. And there was just as much chance of it failing as there was of it succeeding.

And those weren't the kind of odds I wanted to bet on anymore.

CHAPTER 10

Poseidon

*E*lyse was struggling. I'd tried everything I could think of to find Catina, to figure out where X might have taken her.

But I had no idea where else to look. X couldn't go to Mount Olympus, so he had to be here on Earth. I'd covered all the abandoned islands where cyclops and other creatures used to live.

And I found nothing.

The Underworld didn't make sense unless Catina was dead, which I wasn't willing to accept. I didn't want Elyse to think that way, either. Why would X take the human and kill her? He'd have done it in front of Elyse for maximum torture, so I held on to hope.

But the more time that passed without Catina

returning, the more Elyse blamed herself in one way or another, because she hadn't been able to save her.

On Wednesday morning, Ares arrived at my apartment. He didn't just appear like the gods usually did. He knocked on my door as if he respected my privacy. I appreciated that. Lately, he'd shown a different side of himself, one very different from the image we all had of him. He tried to be a better god, and I admired his effort.

"Beer? Soda? Milk?" I asked, opening my fridge. The shelves were filled with all sorts of drinks and a half-eaten red velvet cake. I'd tried a piece at a café the other day and fell in love. Of all the human foods I'd tasted, this dessert had to be the closest to ambrosia, so I'd bought the entire cake from the store.

"No, thanks. I want to talk to you about Elyse," Ares started. "She's not coping well with her friend's kidnapping."

"I know." I shut the fridge door. "Not sure how else to help her."

"I've done what I can too." Ares stood in the living room, his hands hanging by his side, his shoulders rigid. "But you need to step it up a notch."

His face changed when he talked about her. His eyes brightened, his voice filled with excitement.

"You care about her," I ventured.

He nodded once and folded his arms, defensive, his chin lifting. But I wasn't going to attack him. I understood he saw something in her that reflected a part of himself. She did that for all of us. Touched part of us, connected with us, made us reflect on who we were.

It was one of the reasons I didn't mind that she was with Apollo anymore. Elyse was the type of person who made you like yourself again, just because of who you became in her presence. She never asked anything more of me from you than to be myself. And at the heart of it, she wanted love and happiness. As simple as that. I had every intention of making her smile every single day.

"What do you think I should do?" I needed Ares's advice. We were all in this together, so we might as well team up already.

"I think you ought to take her out, do something with her that's not what you usually do." Ares tilted his head to the side but held my gaze. "It's just a thought. I don't know how you two are. But I can tell she likes you a lot. So maybe if we all spend more time with her will help take the edge off her anxiety until we find a way to find X. Apollo found a so-called witch to see if she can find a locator spell for Catina. I might reach out to the Oracle for any insight. You need to help Elyse through this time as well, keep her safe in case X returns."

"Of course." His caring suggestion surprised me, and I enjoyed this new Ares more than the old version. "I like that idea. Appreciate the advice."

He gave me a curt nod of his head and turned to the front door to leave.

"Ares," I called.

He stopped at the entrance and looked at me over his shoulder.

"I might have been wrong about you."

"Thanks," he drawled in a tone that might have been sarcastic.

But I took it at face value. After he left, I called Heracles.

"How do I make Elyse feel special?" I asked, hating how silly I sounded for asking Heracles but also excited to bring joy back to Elyse's life during such a shitty time. "I want to do something humans understand."

"You're asking me about this?" Heracles asked.

"You know her best," I explained. "And you've lived on Earth long enough to be familiar with their customs. I need your help."

Heracles chuckled. "I never thought I'd hear that from any of my uncles. Take her out on a date. Flowers, dinner, the whole thing. Not just sex, but something that shows you care about her."

I'd give his suggestion a try. The whole partnering thing was so different for us gods. We all slept around with whomever we were drawn to and thought nothing more of it, but *dating* seemed so much more different for humans. Maybe because they lived for such a short time. They had something to lose, so they loved hard and deep. Needing that soul-felt connection to bring out their powerful emotions.

"How have you spent so much time with Elyse and not fallen for her?" I wondered.

Heracles was my nephew, but I knew so little about him, and I regretted that now. There were many things I could have spent my time doing other than being the mediator between my two brothers. But it wasn't too late to rectify my past mistakes.

"I only have one love, Uncle," he replied. "Megara was my person. And after her, I just don't want anyone else."

Heracles and Megara had been in love a long, long time ago. After the death of his children and wife, he chose to remain on Earth without them instead of living on Mount Olympus. And I pitied him for living alone this long.

"I never knew I could be this drawn to someone until I met Elyse, so never say never." That was a human saying I'd heard on television, and it seemed appropriate here. "You can't be alone forever either."

Elyse made me feel so real and raw. I had no clue how to voice the words to her, but the promise I'd make her echoed in my heart. A promise to be hers.

When I thought about my emotions for Elyse, I understood how Heracles had devoted himself to Megara. I never understood it before, but Elyse was the type of woman I'd sacrifice eternity for just so we'd have a few years more together. And Heracles had lost his wife, so living in Mount Olympus would just remind him of what he'd lost.

"Thank you," I finally said, after asking one or two more questions about human dating customs.

"Any time," Heracles reassured with cheer in his voice, and I couldn't remember the last time he'd sounded so pleased to chat with me. "I mean it."

I nodded, even though he couldn't see me, because I didn't know what else to say. Then I hung up the phone.

A date? Maybe it wasn't so bizarre. The more I thought about it, the more I couldn't wait to try it out.

When I picked Elyse up later that evening, I carried red roses with me. She opened the door, and her eyes widened at the flowers then she smiled in a way I rarely saw. Pride tickled a spot deep in my heart I hadn't known existed.

"These are beautiful." She accepted the roses and smelled them, her eyes closing as she did. If I could make time stand still, I'd do it in that moment where she seemed at ease. Her mouth curled upward, and she breathed easier. "I'll be right back."

She disappeared into the kitchen. A moment later, she appeared with a water filled vase, and she arranged the flowers inside.

"Thank you," she beamed, turning to me with a smile. "I can't remember the last time anyone bought me flowers."

She wore a little black dress with a scooping neckline, along with black high heels, and her hair was loose for a change. It hung to her hips, and I wanted to run my fingers through it, grab handfuls of the stuff.

"Where are we going?" she asked. "You look sexy."

"Thanks." I'd found a black suit with a sky-blue shirt and a blue tie—the lady who'd sold it to me had told me the outfit matched my eyes.

I teleported us near the classy restaurant where I'd booked a reservation. I led Elyse to a table near the back, and we drank champagne and ate food that was meant to be art, not eaten. Slowly, I watched Elyse relax, and for the first time that night, I sat back, breathing easy, seeing she'd let down her guard to enjoy herself.

"This is such a great idea." She scooped a spoonful of lychee ice cream into her mouth, then glanced around the restaurant. The place was full. Nearby sat an old couple, eating side by side, one glass of wine each, and bent over their meals. Near the large mullioned window that overlooked the street, a group of young women giggled loudly while businessmen at the bar kept glancing over in their direction. A musician sat in front of a grand piano, filling the room with a soft tune. Close to him was a small lounge area with embroidered pillows on couches.

"It's not something the gods do very often, I'm guessing." Elyse's voice drew my attention back to her.

Had she noticed how many times I shifted in my seat and fixed my collar?

"No," I admitted. "I feel lost, in all honesty."

Elyse laughed, the sound like a caress over my skin. "Well, you're doing a great job." She finished her dessert, and I adored the way she licked the spoon, how her tongue flicked out to catch a drop over her lower lip. If we were anywhere else, I would've leaned closer and licked it from her mouth. Instead, I drank my whiskey and smiled.

"How are you?" I probed.

She shrugged, pushing a piece of fruit around in her bowl. "I guess I'm coping. I can't decide if I'm sure she's dead or if I'm upset we haven't found her yet."

I reached across the table and took her hand in mine. Her hand seemed fragile and so soft. The complete opposite of the fierce warrior inside her. I eyed the black tendrils on her skin from where X had bitten her, and she didn't flinch as if in pain. The mark sure took a while to heal.

"She's not dead," I stated. "X wouldn't take her just to kill her somewhere else. He wants to put on a show."

Elyse pursed her lips. "Then why can't we find her? If he's so set on me coming after him, if this is some kind of trap, we should have been able to find her by now, right? She's nowhere, Poseidon. Why is X keeping her?"

"Okay." But I was convinced Catina remained alive. I didn't know what game X was playing, but it wasn't over yet. He'd done this for a reaction. And he'd get one. By Zeus, we'd obliterate him for doing this to Elyse, to her friend.

"I don't know what to make of this," she continued. "I mean, Persephone told me Hades isn't in on this. But I don't get how it happened. How does he know me, how does X know where to hit me?"

"You forget Hades and X both live in a place where the Fates often spend time. They can see a lot more than you think. He probably knew all about you long before any of this happened."

Elyse sighed, her shoulders curling forward in defeat. "So, what now?"

"We don't give up," I said, giving her hand a gentle squeeze. "And I think Persephone's right."

She frowned. "Really? You don't think Hades has anything to do with this either?"

I shook my head. My brother was a lot of things, but he wasn't a monster, and the more I thought about all the lives X had taken, the more I knew it couldn't have been Hades. I hadn't seen what he did before I'd arrived, but Apollo told me Hades had killed Elyse to save her soul before X could kill her. If Hades meant to do harm, he wouldn't have done that. Part of me beamed with joy that my brother wasn't responsible for the atrocities committed by X. After everything we'd gone through, I intended to get my brother back, make good on our relationship.

"I think Hades is lost and confused, and that has

serious repercussions, so, yes, I believe Persephone," I mused. "My brother has been cheated into a life that makes him the bad guy. But if you really get to know him, you'll realize he's still a god. Not the devil."

I couldn't believe I was advocating for my brother, especially since I knew he cared for her. And I was sure she returned his feelings. But I had already shared her with two other men. What was a third?

And Hades deserved to be happy. After everything done to him, by me as well as others, he deserved some kind of happy ending. Even if that was with the same person bringing me *my* happy ending.

Even if it meant sharing a little more of Elyse than I thought I'd have to when this all started.

We were all here to save the world. In the meantime, we'd found love. Would that love be forever? With a human? I didn't know—Elyse was different. But it made sense what Heracles meant when he'd said he wanted no one else after losing his wife.

Could Elyse be the Megara for the rest of us?

CHAPTER 11

Elyse

I couldn't sleep. Usually, I had no problem crashing once my head hit the pillow, given how hard I trained, and I looked forward to the relief of relaxing, especially considering how much happened in my life.

Tonight, I couldn't switch off my brain. My thoughts swirled around Hades. Poseidon was the second deity to tell me Hades wasn't to blame for X's actions. I couldn't believe he wasn't completely involved when X was meant to be a part of him. What was I missing? Or had my initial suspicions that X had broken free come true? But if that was the case, why wasn't Hades bringing his rage down on him?

A big part of me wanted him to be a good guy. But now both Poseidon and Persephone had told me Hades had been innocent through it all, I struggled to wrap my mind around everything we'd been through.

I'd hoped he wasn't the villain here.

Everyone had misunderstood Hades. Everyone thought he was the personification of the devil, the Greek version of the person who presided over hell itself. But they were wrong. Hades was just another god, and the Underworld happened to be his turf.

To some, it was like saying being an executioner was just a job. It didn't make sense to everyone.

Hades wasn't the devil in my book. I saw him differently. But I still grappled to understand how he'd turned his back on X and pretended his actions were fine. I fought my entire life to protect the innocent, to not sit back, because it was too hard or whatever his excuse was, so that was where we differed.

How did that make him a good guy?

I climbed out of bed, since it was clear I wouldn't fall asleep anytime soon, and I sauntered across my dark room to the window. Pulling open the curtain, I stood there and stared out over the sleeping city, shrouded in dark and tried to find more darkness. X threw off an oppressive feeling as if it was a living, breathing thing, not merely the absence of light. And where there was darkness so thick you could barely breathe, there had to be Death.

And this time, Catina would be there, too. Though I couldn't understand why X was hiding. Why take my friend and vanish? Why not confront me and fight already? The fucking ass probably enjoyed torturing me, and his hatred went beyond just finishing me off. Destroying me was a personal vendetta, or some fucked-up shit only a monster like X could comprehend.

But no matter how hard I reached out with my newfound power, the energy humming down my arms, I couldn't sense X. So how the hell was I meant to find Catina? It'd been a long time since X had killed, and I should have been happy about that. But I wasn't. I hated that everything had changed, that yet again, X had the upper hand. And I was completely in the dark about his intentions, leaving me so high-strung I couldn't function or sleep. Frustration hammered through me, twisting in my chest so tightly, I was ready to explode. My eyes prickled at how helpless I felt, and I curled my fists, my fingers digging into the fleshy part of my palm until it hurt. Anything to stop the guilt gnawing on my insides.

Fighting I could do but sitting around waiting killed me.

Every time I became stronger, X did something else to stay one step ahead.

I wanted this to end. I needed my friend back.

Maybe the best way to deal with this was to talk to Hades myself. I hadn't spoken with him in a long time, and I hadn't ever asked him directly what this was all about. It was time I stopped listening to others and confronted him.

When I walked back to the bed and found my phone on the nightstand, it showed two in the morning. It was even later than I had thought, as I'd been up half the night.

The itch to know what was going on intensified. I had to speak to Hades or I'd stir and pace around all night. And I was sure he'd make time to see me even though it was late.

I tried not to think too hard about what it would look like if I arrived at his house at this hour. This wasn't a booty call, after all. And I wouldn't let him think it was.

I got dressed in jeans, a tee, and my boots, climbed in my car, and drove to the bad area of town where he was holed up. Two burned-out cars lined the street and junk filled a house I passed, while two other homes were boarded up and graffitied. The single overhead streetlight flickered, threatening to go out. Shadows crowded this place, the homes shrouded in darkness. I stretched out my energy to search for X but found nothing.

Hades said he lived out here so people would leave him alone.

But his actions were more than enough to make that happen, anyway. He wasn't exactly an approachable guy. Yet the irony wasn't lost on me how I kept finding myself drawn to him, and I somehow suspected Hades received godly visitors anyway—even living out here.

I parked a few houses down from his rundown home, its lawn overgrown, and the trees standing over the property like sentinels. I was cloaked by the night. I got out of the car and quietly closed the door, feeling like I was an intruder.

Before I reached his house, the front door opened and I froze, stepping to the side out of instinct. I stood hidden against thick shrubs, my form melting into the shadows, and I watched.

Persephone emerged from Hades's house. He followed her. His face was grim, and she didn't turn to kiss him. But my heart beat in my throat, and my skin grew hot underneath the layers of clothes I'd put on.

Jealous. I was jealous Persephone had been with Hades at this time of night. And pissed off. Who knew what they'd been doing in there? They had so much history, and he loved her once, he'd said. Maybe he still did?

I squeezed my eyes shut and ground my teeth. She was here because the Underworld was falling apart. And she was the Queen of Darkness, wasn't she? She had a right to talk to him, anyway. It wasn't as if I had some kind of claim on him. Not only were we not together in any way, but I wasn't exclusive with any of the men in my life. I could hardly expect them to be exclusive to me.

God, what was I even saying? I was talking about exclusivity when I didn't even know if what happened between Hades and me had ever been more than just sex.

As I watched Persephone, she disappeared. The gods tended to do that. It wasn't as weird as it used to be. Hades took a deep breath, his chest rising and falling with the sigh, and he started to walk back into the house when he froze mid-stride.

He swung toward me, his eyes searching the darkness.

"Elyse," he said, even though there was no way he could see me. It made me feel like an idiot, like I was a stalker hiding in the bushes. Like a teenage girl spying on a guy I'd crushed on, and my cheeks fired up with heat. I considered running away, but that would be worse. He knew I was here; plus, my car was a couple of houses down and he'd eventually see it.

When I stepped out, his face softened. "I can feel your power." His voice was low, and something was different about him. He wasn't as closed off or aggressive, as usual. Something about him was almost forthcoming. "You've become so strong."

I walked toward him, my chin up, refusing to look as silly as I felt. "I need to talk to you." My palms started to sweat, so I tucked them into my pockets.

Hades nodded. "And I have to chat with you too. I'm glad you came."

Really? At this time of night? His words shouldn't have made me feel as warm as they did, but I was searing like a goddamn sun on the inside. He stood back and let me walk into the house first, and my skin sizzled as I passed him. We hadn't even touched, and I'd already reacted to him. He followed me, closing the door behind us.

"Coffee?" he asked.

Look at him, hosting me as if he were a regular human. It was endearing. But I shook my head. "Just water, please."

I didn't feel like anything, but now I was in Hades's presence, my throat grew dry. Something about him got to me. I couldn't figure out what it was, but butterflies swarmed in my stomach, and I kept studying the way he stood so tall, how well he filled out his black shirt. Hell, I'd missed his company. But I had to remind myself I was here to find a way to help Catina as Hades might know something.

He poured water from the tap, not the fridge, so I assumed he didn't have filtered water. And I was fine with that. The glass he handed me was crystal, the kitchen countertops marble, and I was sure the embellishments were pure gold. This place only looked like a dump from the outside.

On the inside, it truly was the residence of a god. Everything was pristine and could easily be at home on Mount Olympus.

"I'm curious. Why'd you come over now?" he questioned after I took a few sips of my water, and I leaned against the counter.

I stared at the glass in my hand. "I want to know the truth."

"About what?"

This new side of him surprised me. He was raw and vulnerable. I'd never seen him like this. What was happening between us? Or was this something that had taken place between him and Persephone? I expected him to flip his switch at any moment, to be angry, to shout at me.

Or to fuck me.

With him, it could go either way, though the latter thought only fueled the flames engulfing me, and I cursed myself for placing that image in my mind. Who was I kidding? It was there already because anything to do with Hades left me powerless, no matter how much I fought him.

"About X," I finally responded, meeting his bright eyes missed nothing. And they were so filled with emotion, they always showed exactly what he thought.

But tonight, he was difficult to read, as if he'd mastered hiding his emotions, or was he just playing aloof around me? And yet here I was thinking about sex with him—while he was the calm one for a change.

"Let's sit down," Hades said, heading out of the kitchen, expecting me to follow. This brusqueness was a little closer to what I knew about him.

I followed him to the living room. He sat on the edge of a chaise lounge, then shifted several times as if unable to find a comfortable spot. I took the couch opposite him, still clutching my water. It was crazy how much distance was between us now, after everything we'd done together. I half-preferred it when he was demanding, taking what he wanted. I understood it better.

This careful version of Hades was a stranger to me, and in a weird way, I craved the way he used to be for more than familiarity. Hell, this distance shit made me crave him because I was like that spying schoolgirl outside hiding in the bush. And my cheeks heated once more.

"I just heard about Catina," he murmured softly. "Your friend."

So that was what Persephone had been doing here...but no one else had told Hades about the kidnapping? Well, I'd been so lost in my own sorrow, it hadn't occurred to me to contact him, either. Maybe if I had, he might have been able to help Catina more somehow, but in all honesty, part of me figured if he was going to do something about X, he'd have done it already. Yet knowing he and Persephone had talked about something important made me feel better. It was no indication they hadn't slept together afterward, but Hades wasn't wearing the sheen of a satisfied man.

"I only found out tonight. I didn't know." Hades really did look apologetic, the corners of his mouth turned downward, shadows shifted beneath his eyes.

"How could you let this happen?" I blurted out. I hadn't meant to come across as accusing, but I was, all the frustration and grief pushing the words out. "How could you let any of it happen? My friend is in mortal danger because of X."

He sighed. "Look, I realize he's a problem. I've known it for a while, especially once the souls he consumed didn't go to the Underworld. But I hoped if I pretended that everything was fine, it would be."

"You thought it'd just go away? And now my friend is in danger! Where the hell is he hiding her?" My voice climbed.

He paused for a long time, the corners of his mouth tightening, and when he let out a long exhale, I sighed, well aware he didn't like the answer. Which meant I wouldn't either.

"I can occasionally sense him but not his precise location. He's somehow shielded himself from me. And I have no idea where he'd hide on Earth, or even what his interests are. We rarely talked back in the Underworld. Even the Fates couldn't tell me anything about his whereabouts."

"Fuck. Nothing ever works out so easily," I seethed, biting my tongue to stop myself from screaming, as it seemed X was running rings around us.

"You're telling me. I see now it was wishful thinking on my part to ignore him for so long. I bet you won't believe me, but I never meant for anyone to get hurt. I know I'm a son of a bitch, but I don't actually believe in meaningless violence."

His actions over the past months directly contradicted what he'd just said. He'd killed me, for God's sake. But somehow, looking at his face when he spoke, seeing how raw he was, how truly sorry he seemed, I couldn't help but believe him.

And if this was how he felt about Catina being taken, if he was upset about the lives stolen by X, killed so their souls wouldn't end up where they belonged, it was the proof I'd been looking for to believe he was a good guy.

Knowing he wasn't the villain, warmth spread throughout my chest at the reality. But if he was on our side then we needed his help.

I stood, set my half-empty water glass on the coffee table, and crossed the living room. Hades looked unsure when I approached him. He stood as well, ready to receive whatever I planned to dish out. He stared at me with uncertainty, but he never backed away. We'd fought so often that if I attacked, he likely wouldn't have been shocked.

When I was in front of him, I stood on my toes, put my hand around the back of his neck, and pulled him down for a kiss.

Whatever he'd thought I was going to do, it wasn't this. My kiss had caught him by surprise. His body went rigid, as if he wasn't sure this was real.

But I kept my lips pressed to his, and a moment later he relaxed, softening. He wrapped his arms around my body, pulling me against him. We plastered together, his strength enveloping me, his scent melting me with desire. He kissed me properly, and I found the man I'd been with before.

He was sensual, tender, but his power didn't carry the lust that usually came with it. This was more about connecting, about being on the same page.

About caring for each other for more than what we could gain physically.

And I liked this new version of him. Actually, I loved seeing this part of Hades.

I adored that he showed his real self to me.

"How does a cup of coffee sound?" He broke away from me and headed into the kitchen. "If we sit outside, we can probably spot a constellation or two."

It felt strange talking to Hades so normally, with us not fighting, but I loved his company. And picturing us doing ordinary things left me jittery with excitement. It shouldn't have, but he affected me beyond physical attraction. I wanted more of him, the god, the man he was right now.

Plus, I didn't have the heart to tell him Chicago's celestial landscape was almost invisible, obscured behind the strong glow of the city's streetlights and buildings at night. I'd read somewhere that this city was one of the most light-polluted places in the world, which was sad. But I was with Hades, a god, so anything was possible, right?

"Yes to coffee." I smiled to myself, hopeful this was a change in the right direction for Hades and me.

Soon enough, he offered me a cup of coffee with a

dollop of cream, just how I liked it, and took my hand in his. His large palm swallowed mine, and our fingers interlaced. Such a small gesture but my stomach twirled with excitement from the strength of his hold and the way he held me tight like he had no plans of letting go. I glanced up to look at him, and his eyes crinkled at the edges when he smiled. He had the kind of face I could imagine gracing the front of a magazine, where I'd stare at him for hours wondering if someone so handsome could exist, not to mention the soulfulness in his eyes. Except, us standing here was real, and he looked at me with a longing that weakened my knees.

"Let's head out," he said. "To get some fresh air."

Before we took a step, the world around us shimmered, then darkened. Within a heartbeat, we stood outside in the night where a soft wind buffeted against me, curling under my hair.

I looked out from the cliff's edge, over a canyon with a river. Shadows dwelled below like night creatures, resembling the shapes of monsters. I should be terrified of what might be hiding in the shadows, but I wasn't scared. Not in Hades's company, despite our rocky relationship and his unpredictability. Overhead, an abundance of star clusters and galaxies stared down on us, their brightness lighting up the spectacular heavens.

"We're in the Grand Canyon?"

"Yes." Hades took a drink of his coffee and guided

me to sit down on a rock ledge that resembled a bench. "This is as close to the beauty of Mount Olympus as I can take you. And it has a wicked view of the sky." He pointed upward. "That's the Milky Way, and that faint pulsing star is Mars. It's a representation of Ares. He reminds anyone who listens to him."

I laughed, because I could picture Ares doing that. I set my cup down near my feet and studied the star that burned a little brighter, larger than the rest. "Do you have a star?"

He chuckled and placed his cup down. "I have the whole Underworld." His voice dripped sarcasm, but he laughed it off, and I left it at that, not wanting to discuss such dark things. Tonight shouldn't have made me smile or laugh because my friend was still out there. And I had every intention of finding her. Now, with Hades by my side, we'd track her down in no time. I'd been drawn to the man from the moment I first met him, to enjoy this new side of him.

"See that glimmer over there, up on the right?" He leaned closer, not enough to touch me, not yet, but the hairs on my arms shifted. He pointed, and I followed the line of sight of his outstretched index finger.

"Yeah?"

"That's the prancing horse constellation." His breath blew against my neck. My heart pounded, lunging into my throat. I tried to swallow, but my voice grew husky.

"I see it." I breathed hard.

"When Saturn's in the right position and you look at it sideways, the planet is seen to be riding the horse."

I tilted my head but couldn't find the rider. "It's gorgeous."

Hades's lips were on my neck, and I arched my spine, bursting with tingles. I leaned closer, my hand on his leg, gripping his thigh. His fingers stroked my lower back, drawing me against him.

"You react so beautifully to my touch" He kissed my brow and slid a finger under my chin, lifting my face to his, to meet his lips as he grazed my mouth. Softly at first, tender and smooth, and I closed my eyes, trembling. I was lost, floating under his strong hands holding me in place, yet his kiss was light and so damn sensual. I clenched my thighs as arousal rekindled through me.

He cupped my face and his passion intensified, his mouth pressing against mine, his tongue surging forward. And I took him in, tasting his offering. The groan in his chest rolled through me.

I moaned, placing a flat hand on his rock-hard chest, feeling his thundering heartbeat.

But he broke our kiss and simply collected me tight into his embrace. I burned on the inside, needing, craving, dying for more. But as much as I contemplated straddling him and ripping off his clothes, I also sensed tonight wasn't about lust with Hades. He wanted companionship, and a small part of me appreciated that for a change.

His breaths eased. "Why did somebody not teach me the constellations, and make me at home in the starry heavens, which are always overhead, and which I don't half know to this day?"

That didn't sound like something Hades would say. I pulled myself up and stared at him, arching a brow. "Is that a question?"

"Yes, by Thomas Carlyle. He's a Scottish philosopher. Sometimes I need to remind myself the answer I seek is right in front of me."

Hades always surprised me, and I would never have guessed he read the works of a philosopher.

He wrapped me in his arms once again, not letting me stray for long, and I nestled my head on his shoulder. A man who'd influenced me so much against my back felt primal and right. We sat there, star gazing, holding each other. I desired him and fell even deeper for him with each moment that passed. More than anything, I hoped this was the start of a deeper relationship between us. So, I pushed aside the doubts, refusing to even entertain them tonight.

CHAPTER 12

Ares

I was growing sick and tired of this game. X had disappeared with Catina and no matter where I looked, I couldn't find him. None of us could.

The son of a bitch had vanished as if he never existed, but on the bright side, I hadn't sensed him consuming innocents, so what the fuck was he up to?

My life would have been a hell of a lot easier without him. But then I wouldn't have met Elyse. I had mixed feelings about the fucker being here.

Finding Catina meant everything to Elyse, so I intended to help her track down her friend. And I'd searched everywhere I could think of and where I thought would make sense. Poseidon and Apollo were doing the same.

But X was nowhere to be found. And I was running

out of ideas. How was I going to find Catina? She had no power signature of her own, being a human. And I should've been able to find X with all the darkness that surrounded him, but there was nothing. It frustrated the hell out of me. As gods, we could reach out and sense similar beings, but X was untraceable. He was damn smarter than I'd given him credit for, and it meant I shouldn't underestimate him. Fuck, he pissed me off.

Wherever he was, perhaps he wasn't within the confines of the city.

It wasn't the first time I'd considered that. Poseidon searched in obscure places, trying to trace X back all the way back to Greece. But those islands were long abandoned by the gods, and it seemed unlikely X would have gone there. It was too easy of a spot for him to hide. Still, Apollo scoured mountains and isolated locations and caves.

That was what I was looking for—something that didn't seem straightforward—somewhere that wasn't easy to find. X was upping his game because Elyse gave him hell. He wasn't going to make this easy for her to figure out. Or for any of us. And the bastard more than likely saw this as a game, and I bet that was why he'd kidnapped Catina, to toy with Elyse, drive her insane. But had he counted on all of us gods taking her side to bring him down?

And I wanted to be the hero who got Catina back.

I had no idea if Catina was even alive. We all kept

telling Elyse not to lose hope, that X wouldn't have killed her. None of us knew for sure, but I remained convinced that Catina was still breathing.

For one, X wanted to draw Elyse out in a certain way and get rid of her. She made his life hard. I wasn't sure what he was trying to achieve, but Elyse was stopping him from doing it.

For another, if X had just killed Catina and moved on, he wouldn't have disappeared. He'd be going on and on, killing humans, consuming souls. He wouldn't be lie low.

What exactly he was doing to that human was a different story, but I refused to give it thought or bring such worries to Elyse for the moment.

And I was sure one hell of a fight would ensue.

Which was why I needed to determine what was going on so we could jump into it already and get this done. Elyse could take care of herself, no doubt about it. She was a fucking skilled fighter.

But I wanted to spare her the risk of dying another time and protect her. Because she only had one life left before her final death.

And I didn't think I'd be able to handle it if she were dead for good. Eliminated from our world. Not now I'd just found her, started to connect with her, had her see me for who I really was. I needed more time to get to know her. I didn't know how long I'd have with her—she was godly in a lot of ways but still human. I didn't know how long "forever" would be with her. And thinking about the future hurt my head, reminding me of some of Zeus's words about gods not falling for mortals, as it came with consequences. And now I suspected he meant the heartbreak, the agony of watching them die—knowing it was coming while there was shit I could do to change that fate.

But I'd make sure her life was as long as possible while I had her.

Did it seem selfish? Maybe. But sometimes, that was love.

I paddled on the edge of Lake Michigan, the sky cloaked in clouds, when the ripple of a familiar power licked the length of my spine. I turned and spotted Apollo not too far off. He stood on the edge of the water, staring north.

When I approached him, he glanced my way and his expression changed from one of concentration to a smile. The gods used to hate me, but recently, we'd become allies, if not friends. And it was a welcome change to not be on guard each time I crossed paths with them. Another reason coming to Earth for Elyse had worked out—creating bonds with the gods in ways I'd never thought possible. For so long, I accepted my fate as the lone wolf, the one they criticized and blamed. Now, the reprieve from their taunts offered a calming relief. A welcome change I intended to hold on to, as I'd missed being one of them.

"What're you doing here?" he asked, clapping his palm into mine and bumping me with his shoulder.

"Same as you," I said. "Trying to track down that fucker."

Apollo's hands briefly clenched. "I don't even know where to keep searching. I've checked everywhere I can think of, and I'm sure we've all covered spots the others have already inspected. We must look like fools running around, hunting for X. I bet he's having a fat laugh."

"He can laugh," I growled, bristling with anger. "He won't be amused for much longer."

Apollo sighed. "At this rate…"

"What fucks me up about this is that we don't know what to expect," I broke in, not letting Apollo go on with a thought that couldn't lead to anywhere good. "He's usually so damn predictable, it was almost a sin we couldn't stop him. But now? I've no idea what game he's playing, and that pisses me off."

"Yeah, this is a big mess," Apollo agreed. He gathered his blond hair together as if he wanted to tie it up but let it go again. I'd get so fucking irritated with hair like that. I kept mine shaved as short as possible. It was more practical in a fight and didn't give the enemy anything to grab on to.

"We all know he wants her," I said. "And he wants her bad. What if we miss something and he gets to her?" Just saying those words churned my gut because they came from a place of fear. The dread I'd lose the one good thing that'd happened to me in too long.

"Over my dead body," Apollo growled. It was a

funny statement coming from a god who couldn't die. But maybe that was the point he was trying to make.

"He wants to take her out for good."

"He won't get his hands on her soul," Apollo pointed out. "He just can't, not with Zeus's magic in her veins."

"I hope you're right. But she's the last fighting Lowe. The others in her family line don't even know who they are anymore. And if she's dead—wherever her soul may go—she'll be out of X's way. That's ultimately what the son of a bitch is after. So what's his intention with her gone? Devour as many innocents as possible? Rule over Earth? Grow so powerful, we wouldn't be able to stand in his way?"

Apollo nodded without answering. We both knew I was right. But we had to stop this from happening. Without Elyse, X would run rampant in the streets, killing for fun, consuming souls because he felt like it. Because he was part of Hades, we couldn't do anything about him directly.

It was a gigantic loophole Zeus should have worked out before he decided it would be fun to fuck with Hades.

But I guess we didn't always see the shit we caused before it was too late. I'd learned that years ago when I'd still been fucking around and impregnating women left and right. Not that I regretted the sex, but the kids were all demigods who strived to be like me. That was a disaster in and of itself; I didn't even want to think about.

Let's just say I was a hell of a role model.

"If we don't find X, Catina might die but Elyse will be safe," Apollo mused.

I saw where he was going with this. And he was right. The flipside was that if we found Catina, X might kill Elyse and the world would end. But if he took the human out, what stopped him coming for Elyse again and again?

"We can't stop looking now," I began. "She's already taken a massive knock to her self-esteem because she couldn't stop X from taking the human."

"That's what X wanted," Apollo growled, the bridge of his nose creasing.

Of course, he was right there. It was exactly what he'd wanted. When you intended to throw someone off their game, you hit them where it hurt. It was what Hera did to Zeus when she'd tried to eliminate Heracles so long ago. That plan blew up in her face, and somehow the family feud had died down a little, but that was how you played dirty.

And X was playing filthy as fuck.

"We have to keep her safe, then," Apollo said after we stood together in silence for a while, staring into the cloudy sky. "Getting Catina back, doing what we can, isn't negotiable. We have to make sure X doesn't succeed in whatever he's trying to do. But by Zeus, the asshole is making life difficult for us."

Hell, he was, but it was okay. This meant there was

going to be a fight, and goddamn, I loved a good battle. I itched for combat.

"We just have to find X," Apollo interrupted my thoughts. "If we don't find him, this whole thing is pointless, and we'll seem pathetic because we couldn't figure it out."

That was true, too. We'd look like idiots if we couldn't find him. Three gods unable to find Death.

The water in the lake started to bubble.

"What's happening over there?" I asked, pointing to the middle of the lake.

He glanced over his shoulder and frowned. Both of us stared at the spot. Darker clouds crowded overhead, and the water turned as black as ink, spreading outward like tentacles.

"It's X," I snarled.

Apollo opened his mouth to answer, but he didn't get the chance. X appeared before Apollo could say anything and floated across the water in his black form, a dark fog lingering behind him as if he wore it as a cape. No sign of Catina.

I tensed, curling my hands into fists, ready for a fight. Though, why the fuck would X come to us?

Apollo mirrored my posture, and we glared at the monster. My armor appeared as my power flared and Apollo was suddenly surrounded by light as if he were glowing. We were going to take X down here and now. Finish this messed-up shit once and for all.

When he reached us, X smiled, revealing his

yellowing teeth under thin lips. God, he was an ugly motherfucker. His teeth were sharp and dripping, as if he salivated for food. His eyes were filled with what I could only call hellfire. But he didn't scare me. I thrummed with energy, buzzing to charge.

"Look at you two. Pathetic," he growled, his voice half-human, half-grunting like a wild animal. But he sounded almost bored.

"Bring it on, asshole," Apollo bit out.

X laughed, the sound grating over my nerves. I was over his shit.

"What's so funny?" I sneered.

"The two of you thinking you can make a difference. But I still have the human and attacking me won't help. If you want the human, bring Elyse. It's a fair trade, no?"

"Fuck that," Apollo snarled.

X shrugged, but stared at us unblinking.

What the hell was his master plan? A simple negotiation or did have something else in mind, like find a way to take out as many humans as possible while he finished Elyse? Or was this some show so we could witness whatever evil disruption he had planned?

"Yes, I didn't think you'd fall for that. But it was worth a try. Pity you won't find where I've hidden her away. And she won't hold on much longer. How will you tell your precious little girl you failed her? I've been hiding right under your noses. You're such a disappointment."

I'd heard enough. I charged X, whipping out my sword, ready to do some serious damage.

But he vanished again, the sun emerging from behind the clouds, the water shimmering quietly like a mirror, as if all of this had been nothing more than a dream.

"Fuck!" Apollo shouted, his voice like thunder.

"He's in the Underworld," I declared.

Apollo stared at me, his eyes narrowing as if putting two and two together. "He can't be. Catina can't survive down there. She's human."

"I don't know how he's doing it, but that's the only place we haven't looked. He can't be on Mount Olympus. I think he just went back home."

"No," Apollo refused. "No way."

"Why don't you just fucking trust me for once?" I snapped. "He said he was right under our noses."

Apollo raised an eyebrow.

"I realize you don't think much of me, but I'm right, and I'm a fucking god just like you. So, swallow your pride and take my side. If I'm wrong, I'll grovel and eat shit."

"Zeus almighty, fine." Apollo shook his head, holding up his hands. "We'll go to the Underworld. You don't have to get your panties in a twist."

"Fuck you and your Earthly sayings." I stalked off, well aware I'd used so many of those stupid sayings when I'd first arrived in Chicago as well, so getting mad at Apollo had nothing to do with him but everything to do with X.

Apollo followed me, his laughter a rumble in the air around us. I tried to ignore him. Because I was a breath away from belting him, but he wasn't the guy I needed to fight.

CHAPTER 13

Elyse

When someone knocked on my door on Saturday evening, I groaned. I suspected Oliver, as he'd always popped over at this time before my life had morphed into a mess, but I didn't need company. I yearned to be alone, to deal with Catina's disappearance in peace without talking about it with anyone.

After I visited Hades the other night, a sense of calm had come over me because I'd started to understand him better, to see he held on to so much anger because he was afraid. And nothing I said could change him, but I'd be there for him, understand him, let him know he wasn't alone. For that reason, I spent the next few hours drinking coffee with him and chatting about the galaxy, the constellations, anything that didn't deal with either of our problems. But after coming home, the reality of Catina's predicament had crashed through me, and I'd moped in my apartment ever since.

I wiped my wet eyes and tightened my hold on my knees in the corner of the couch.

Oliver knew about the missing persons case I'd opened. He found out about it when he'd went to visit Catina at work. I wasn't sure why he'd been looking for her. Maybe, under different circumstances, I'd have been happy about the progression of whatever was happening between them. But her kidnapping was my fault, and it seemed everything I touched I fucked up. Like poor Oliver finding me dead in my apartment and Heracles needing to wipe his mind clean. Now because of me, my best friend was at the mercy of a psychotic monster, and Oliver worried for her. They were all better off without me in their lives.

If Catina liked Oliver, I wanted her to be with him. I wished for them to be happy and for them to have a long future together.

Right now, I just prayed she was still alive.

A second knock sounded at the door, and I ignored it. The gods just appeared in my living room, so it wasn't one of them.

I yearned to be alone, because I felt lost and pathetic that I hadn't been able to help Catina.

A moment later, the air in front of me rippled and

Ares appeared in my living room, larger than life in front of me where I sat on the couch. He wore jeans and a red tee that pulled taut across his strong chest.

"Don't you answer your door?" he asked, gripping his hips.

"Since when do you knock?" I grinned, glad it was him. Of all the gods, he was the one I needed to see. Not because I favored him above the others or anything, but because his goofy attitude, the way nothing was ever super serious with him, was exactly what I needed. Plus, he didn't sit around and grieve with me but rather tried to remind me all wasn't lost, so I thanked the stars it wasn't Oliver at the door.

"Is there a reason you're ignoring the world?" He flopped down next to me then stretched his arm up and put it around my back as if it'd landed there after the stretch. It was a classic jock move and endearing.

I giggled, leaning into him, pressing myself up against him. His body was hot, the heat thawing me where I'd felt cold and forgotten.

"I can't find her," I admitted. "And I feel horrible about it."

Ares hesitated. He looked as if he wanted to say something, but he kept silent. His breathing picked up and he was definitely keeping something from me.

"What is it?" I asked.

The muscles in his neck corded. "I just wish I could do more," he finally said.

I sighed. "You're doing so much already. We'll figure this out, I guess. Or we won't." I scrubbed my face with my hands. "God, I don't know anymore. Before, my mission was simple. Eradicate the monsters, get rid of X. Now I feel as if I'm swimming through a black hole, unsure which direction to go."

Ares put his hand on my cheek. He turned my face toward him so I looked him in the eyes. They were seafoam green, lighter than usual, but no less intense, and I couldn't ignore his handsome features, the strong jawline, the parted lips I wanted against mine.

For a moment, he looked at me with adoration. But it very quickly changed into something deeper. Something hotter. And I responded to the heat that flowed from his body to mine, the way his eyes dragged down to my lips and his fingers curled in my hair, telling me what he wanted without saying a word.

I desired it, too. To escape, to experience of a release—and Ares would give me exactly that. I knew he would.

He kissed me, closing the distance between us, pressing his lips against mine. His mouth and cheeks were as hot as the rest of him. It was as if he burned up, but it wasn't anything like that. Rather, it was the fever of his lust.

Or maybe it wasn't just lust. It seemed more than that. This was different than the first time we'd slept together. When he studied me, I saw his affection for me in his eyes. How had we moved from something that was a giant question mark to something so solid in only a matter of days? He'd been my rock in a time of devastation, turning out to be a different man from whom I'd first met.

But I imagined Ares was like this in every sense. With him, it was all or nothing.

His tongue slid over my lips, and I moaned softly as he tasted me, explored my mouth. His hand slid down my neck, over my collarbone and onto my chest. I expected him to touch my breasts, but he didn't. He stayed just above them, making me ache for his touch without going any farther.

I put my hands on his chest. His pectoral muscles were chiseled, every inch of him was ready for war, and his body was solid under my palms.

Slowly, he drove me down, gently, until I was on my back on the couch. His body hovered above mine. He leaned over me, but he didn't put his weight on me. Even though I could handle it now.

While he kissed me—slowly, sensually, making out —he pressed his hand under my tank top. He ran his hand over my stomach, his rough palm brushing across my skin, and I shivered. But he didn't move to my breast. He didn't touch the skin on fire for him, he didn't tweak my already hard nipples. He caressed me as if merely touching me was enough for him.

The desperation within me climbed, yet I lay victim

to his teases, unable to get enough. Ready to soar through the heavens from his touch and pleasure.

Slowly, he pushed up my shirt, and I lifted my arms. We broke the kiss so he could work the shirt over my head. I wasn't wearing a bra, and his eyes slid over my breasts, my tight nipples. He didn't say anything, and I was glad.

It would have ruined the moment. The rawness of him staring at me with such hunger had me clenching my thighs together, heightening the growing ache for him.

Ares traced my body with his fingertips, following the curve of my ribs to my narrow waist and out to the flare of my hips. He tugged my sweatpants down.

I wasn't wearing panties, either.

"I'm the only one who's naked now," I whispered when he pulled my pants off my ankles.

"Yeah," he breathed, as he grabbed the back of his collar and pulled his tee over his head. He dragged his jeans and jocks down and kicked them off, too. Everything about him was about restraint tonight. He touched me as if he intended to worship my body, not just fuck it.

But he was horny for me. His dick was rock-hard and standing at attention. The tip was wet with precum, and I resisted the urge to lean over and take him into my mouth. Part of me welcomed being the one getting the affection, letting myself drown in something other than my thoughts.

Ares held out his hand, and I put mine in his. He helped me up, and we walked to the bedroom together, naked.

He kissed me when we reached my room, and while he kissed me gently, taking my tongue into his mouth, he guided me to the bed. I climbed onto it, moving away from his touch and his body for only a moment before he followed me.

I lay on my back and Ares covered my body with his, holding himself up with his arms, his cock pressing against my lower abdomen. I shivered when he kissed me again, a chaste passion on the lips before he started moving down my body.

He left a trail of fire down my neck, his fingers tracing my jaw on the other side before moving to my chest. This time, he didn't avoid my breasts. He moved onto the soft skin, kissing and nibbling until I squirmed, desperate for more.

"Please," I moaned. He was driving me crazy, making me wait.

I felt him smile as he kissed me on the mouth again before he moved back down and drew one of my nipples into his mouth. I gasped when he sucked hard. His hands on my breasts, he scraped the nipple with his teeth, flicking it with his tongue, before he moved to the other side.

It made me impossibly wet, and I bucked my hips in a gentle rhythm, eager to take him. To fall completely under his spell.

"You're a work of art," he murmured when he finally moved away from my breasts and down my stomach. My hands were on his shoulders, feeling the muscles under his skin as he moved, leaving a trail of pecks on his way to the V between my legs.

When I opened my legs wide for him, he chuckled. It was a deep sound, delicious. He glanced at me, his eyes almost all pupil and outlined in almost impossible green.

Ares dove between my legs and licked a line from my entrance to my nub. I called out with pleasure when he flicked his tongue over my clit, making me squirm.

"You taste so good," he said, glancing up from between my thighs, his gaze almost hazed over as if he were high.

I didn't have time to answer. He pressed two fingers into me and closed his mouth around my clit. I cried out again, the sensation almost as good as when he pushed into me.

He started moving his fingers in and out while he licked and sucked on my clit and the attention brought me closer and closer to the edge. I hadn't known it could be this intense without actually having sex.

I loved it. The world around us faded away: I writhed under his attention as he spread my legs wider with his free hand. Only Ares and I existed. All I focused on were his fingers as his mouth did deliciously wicked things to my pussy.

A moment later, an explosion ripped through so fast and powerful, I screamed from the orgasm owning me. I toppled over the edge, curling on the bed, crying out as euphoria gripped me. My muscles spasmed, my eyes closed, and I gasped and moaned, losing track of where I was, of everything that haunted me. All that existed right now was Ares and the way he made me feel.

After the orgasm subsided, I lay on the bed in a puddle of sweat, breathing hard, smiling so damn wide my cheeks hurt. Ares crawled up to me, his lips glistening. With his hands on either side of my head, he kissed me. I could taste myself on his mouth, and I loved it.

He lay down next to me and pulled me against him, facing each other.

"I haven't even returned the favor," I noted, though a heavy wave of fatigue pulled through me suddenly. I tucked my head under his chin.

"Tonight isn't about me," he said in a soft voice. "It's all about you."

I was so tired I couldn't keep my eyes open. "What did you do to me?"

He didn't answer. He didn't have to. I knew exactly what he'd done. He'd taken the time to make me feel like I was worth it. Not asking for an orgasm, or even sex, seemed like something so small. But it was selfless, and I couldn't explain to him how much it meant that he'd focused on me tonight.

I was lost, alone, and inconsequential. And he'd

arrived at just the right time and somehow helped me forget about how awful I felt.

Catina was still missing, but we'd find her somehow. There was nothing that could be done. And worrying about it only robbed me of sleep and made me weak.

But it was okay to be weak. Ares was with me, and I knew he'd stand over me, guard me.

I closed my eyes, my hand pressed against his chest. He wiggled his arm under my head, and I curled close to him. Ares held on to me, and I let it all go. The panic, the anger, the helplessness. For now, it was just Ares and I, and I'd let him take care of me for once.

Like he already had.

What had I done to deserve such beautiful people in my life? I didn't know, but I did know that I was grateful for Ares. When I met him, I thought he'd be a waste of my time. I judged him too quickly, remained too preoccupied with doing what I believed was right, when all this time, I had these gods who were ready to pledge themselves to me. Sure, it hadn't been completely clear initially, but I'd also never given them the benefit of the doubt. It took losing my best friend for me to reassess my priorities and see who made a difference in my life. Who was worth keeping at my side.

I'd been wrong about Ares, and I should have let him show me otherwise from the beginning.

Now, he had, time and time again. I didn't know how it was possible to fall so deeply for four different men, but there it was. It wasn't just Apollo and Poseidon and the strange game I played with Hades.

Ares was crawling into my heart, too.

CHAPTER 14

Hades

*W*hat I hated most about being a god was not being able to forget. Sure, I could drink until I was wasted mess who didn't know his own name. But the next day I'd just be sober again, and all this bullshit would still haunt me.

I'd come to Earth to get away from Persephone. The Underworld had become my home, no matter how much I hated it, but I let her have it so we didn't stare at each other for half the year.

There was nothing worse than having to face the woman you knew didn't love you for the centuries you'd been together.

On Earth, forgetting about her had been easy enough. Out of sight, out of mind, that was how the saying went, right? Humans and their damn expressions.

But now she was here. Persephone had decided to come to Earth and taunt me, merely by being around. And no matter how large this place was, it just wasn't big enough for the two of us. I couldn't stop remembering every shitty little detail about our pretend-relationship that had led us both to realize we'd never been cut out for each other.

I grasped Hera had fucked with me, and Persephone had finally decided to stop playing along.

What a joyous fucking day that had been. Not.

I'd been up all night. I hadn't been able to sleep Saturday. At all. I sat on my patio, the shit-ugly outside of my house all around me, and I watched the sunrise as it colored the world after an inky black night.

Thank Zeus, Apollo had decided to find love again. Without his sunlight piercing the overcast clouds, the world had been a pretty dull place. Not that my brother knew Apollo was dating Elyse. It was sure to get him screwed somehow—Zeus was all about pointing fingers and making rules.

But I'd be happy for Apollo while it lasted. It was going to come to an end at some point, for sure.

I wished I could love as easily as Apollo did. If only it was that simple for me. But when your heart got broken the way mine had, you just didn't close your eyes and jump anymore. Because chances were, no one would catch your sorry ass, and you were going to plant yourself face-first in the dirt.

Ask someone who knew from experience.

But I sure desired a bit of company. Even if just to share this glorious sunrise with in the mornings.

I never saw anything like this in the Underworld. The place was drab, dark, beautifully decorated in every fucking shade of gray you could imagine. It was enough to make your mood dull, too.

Up here, I could think, I could breathe, I could feel.

Which wasn't always a good thing.

I shivered when a slice of darkness awoke inside me. I closed my eyes and tried to will the darkness away.

It was X. The fucker was linked to me—he was supposed to be a part of me, almost like my shadow—and I could feel him. I hated that I could. He'd gotten away from me, so he was free to kill, but he hadn't escaped enough that I couldn't feel him anymore. Not where the bastard hid, I just sensed him.

Last time I tried to follow the sensation, it sent me in circles for hours, because the bastard had no intention of letting me know where he hid with Catina. But every now and then, I sensed him stir, as if our link hadn't completely severed.

Talk about straddling both worlds.

I hated knowing when he consumed souls, when he did something unforgivable. All I wanted was to do the job I had been tricked into and live through another damn day.

But I was stuck with this asshole, this murderer, and I had no idea what to do with it.

Elyse had finally come around to seeing I wasn't a villain, but it took her long enough. And of course, why wouldn't she believe the bad stuff? Even if I hadn't been associated with X's misdeeds at all, I wasn't exactly a fun guy to be around. I was moody and messy, and all I wanted from her was sex.

Or rather, the only affection I knew how to show her was lust. The rest was hidden under this ugly mug.

I sighed. How was I going to deal with these feelings for her? Because I'd gone past the point where I could deny them. The other night, when she came to me to find out for herself if I was really okay with all this X shit, I'd shown her a side of me that was damn vulnerable.

That was usually a mistake, showing women you could break.

But there it was. She knew now. She saw that there was more than just the hard outer shell. She'd found out I had a heart in here somewhere.

I was always so macho, I had no idea how to tell her I was terrified of love, that I didn't know what to do when I was around her, that I wished I hadn't fallen for her because I was so worried about getting hurt again.

I was such a fucking pussy even thinking these thoughts, acknowledging I felt something. Part of me just wanted to say, *fuck it all*, and sweep her into my arms and speak my mind. Tell her I wanted her by my side, that I didn't worry about getting my heart torn out and trampled on. But I couldn't do it because I lived with the fear of what I'd already been through.

Elyse flashed in front of me as if my thoughts had conjured her up, and I closed my eyes, letting the memories of her push away the darkness that came with my link to X. I liked how I felt around her. Light. Happy.

Like I could be enough.

But I couldn't accept that. I couldn't be with her. I opened my eyes again, and the warmth disappeared. The darkness returned, and I swore out loud.

"Fuck, fuck, fuck!" I got up and stomped back into the house. What was I supposed to do with this shit? Stopping myself from loving her wasn't working. Zeus knew I tried. But being with her was dangerous. I was strong now—after I'd put myself back together when Persephone had told me I wasn't enough for her. I'd scraped together every sad piece of me that had shattered and rebuilt myself. As best as I could. And maybe I wasn't *enough* for Elyse, considering she had three other men in her life.

I wasn't going to be able to do this again. I sure as fuck didn't want to suffer that humiliation and sorrow again.

I opened the closet and grabbed my leather jacket. It made me look slick, and I appreciated some of the fashions the humans came up with. Leather and weapons were a great combo. Why hadn't the gods thought of it?

Without thinking about where I was going, I closed my eyes and disappeared into a scramble of divine power, shooting through the air, going wherever the wind took me.

When I took form again, I stood outside the training center where Elyse worked out, cloaked in morning light.

Fuck, I couldn't trust myself anymore, could I? Seeing her wasn't what I wanted.

Or maybe it was.

Whatever.

The center was closed, anyway. It was a Sunday. The humans took days off. They had to cherish every moment when they were only alive for so many years.

I was on my way out again when I stopped. Magic danced over my nape, and power called to me.

She was here. The place was shut, but she was in there. I walked to the front door and tested the handle, but it was locked. When I looked through the window, I found her inside, working with weapons I hadn't seen people use in years.

A scythe? That was new.

And pretty damn hot, the way she wielded the thing.

I looked around. There were no humans in sight. And no Heracles or any of the others inside, either.

Elyse was alone. And suddenly, I didn't want to be. So I poofed my way inside the training center. Elyse wasn't the only one who could be somewhere she didn't belong. It made me think of the time I snuck her into the police station to devour her pussy.

What a thrill it had been, and the memory stayed with me.

Every time with her had been exciting.

I stood in the corner, cloaked by the shadows of early morning, and watched her work. The scythe was new, but every time she died, I realized she used something new—like a pattern of regrowth. This addition, I liked.

I didn't know how long she'd been working with the new toy, but she moved as if she knew exactly what she was doing, as if she'd used it for years. She was faster, stronger. More than anything, I'd seen her do this before. She moved around the room with a speed and agility that would easily cause damage, even against the toughest of adversaries.

X would be in trouble if she went up against him.

But he knew that. I could feel it in my bones. He was preparing, just as she was. He wasn't going to go down without a hell of a fight. In fact, he didn't plan to go down at all.

"Elyse," I said, stepping out of the shadows.

She shot toward me, the scythe suddenly at my neck. It wasn't going to kill me, but the power that surrounded her, the aggression behind her attack, was enough to instill fear. I sensed the tendrils of it, trying to claw at my divine power. If I were anything other than immortal, I'd be in all kinds of trouble.

"Don't sneak up on me like that," she reprimanded when she realized who I was. "Jesus, I could have hurt you."

I chuckled. "Not likely. But you would have done damage. You're pretty good with that thing."

She frowned at me. "Why are you so nice lately?"

I shrugged. It was a bad sign that she was skeptical of me being polite. It said a lot about my behavior lately.

Thankfully, she didn't wait for an answer. She put the scythe down, and drank from her water bottle. I watched her. Everything about her was hot and beautiful, and I yearned to be around her always, just because it beat being anywhere else.

"What're you doing here?" I asked. "Isn't it the humans' rest day?"

She smiled. "I'm doing what you're doing."

"What's that?"

"Running away."

Fuck, I was in trouble. She knew me better than I'd thought. And I loved it. She cared enough to know me.

"What are you running away from?" I probed.

She avoided my gaze. "I guess I'm scared I'll fail. I'm scared I won't get Catina back or save anyone. That I'm just ornamental and Zeus made a mistake."

"Zeus doesn't make mistakes," I said bitterly. "No matter what he decides to do, it's always calculated."

I was thinking about him forcing me to go to the Underworld.

Elyse was suddenly in front of me. I didn't know if she moved super-fast, which she could do now, or if she had just walked up to me and I'd been too caught up in my thoughts to notice.

"Don't do that," she demanded.

"What?"

"Don't let someone else dictate who you become."

I waved her away dismissively.

Irritation creasing her brow, and her cute lips pinched tight.

"I'll do whatever the fuck I want," I snarled.

Anger, that was my fallback. I understood rage. It was better than all these other emotions.

"Fine," she said. "Do whatever you want."

She turned away from me and picked up the scythe to continue training. She wasn't even upset I'd snapped at her. She'd accepted me for what I was. An asshole. And I wasn't sure if I ought to feel glad or pissed.

I watched her as she moved through her routine. Then I stepped in front of her and mimicked her movements.

But fury still bled through my veins. Not because of Zeus or Persephone or even X.

I was furious because I was falling harder and harder for Elyse...and I couldn't stop myself.

CHAPTER 15

Ares

I'd contemplated telling Elyse about my hunch that Catina was in the Underworld when I went to see her on Saturday. I wanted her to stop worrying.

But I'd said nothing. How could I get her hopes up if I wasn't sure Catina was really there, or that she'd still be alive? And I didn't want to put Elyse in danger, either. Because it was a fact that she'd go find Catina the moment she suspected where her friend was hidden. With her tenacity, she'd find a way to enter the Underworld. And that worried me.

Not only because it was her job to fight X and protect the humans, but because she felt personally responsible for Catina's disappearance. Plus, Elyse had never been the type to sit back and let a hero take over. Elyse was the furthest thing from a damsel in distress, and that was one of the things that attracted me to her.

I didn't want her to get it in her head she could go to the Underworld, only to find that Catina wasn't there and then X would have her where he wanted her.

Because X left us that little clue from the lake to draw Elyse out, since we weren't doing well enough finding him ourselves. Fucker probably roared with laughter at us. If we sprung a trap he'd set, I'd never forgive myself, and I wasn't taking that risk with Elyse's life.

So instead of telling Elyse about my hunch on Saturday, I'd spent time focusing on her, helping her forget.

My phone rang, and Elyse's name flashed on the Caller ID.

"Hey," I answered with a smile, certain she could hear it.

"Can I see you?" she asked, her voice serious, yet, I sensed no fear.

"Is everything okay? You can tell me now."

She hesitated. "Yeah, I just want to talk."

It was unlike her to be insecure about anything, and even more strange for her to ask for company. But I had to take care of Underworld business first. I'd put anything aside for her, but this was different because it might be the answer she needed.

"I need to look into something first," I said. "I can't

see you right now. I'll come to you as soon as I'm done, okay?"

"Sure," she murmured.

I wasn't certain if she thought I was okay at all—something was up, and it worried me. She wasn't in danger, which was the priority.

I had more important things to focus on that would help her.

After we ended the call, I headed out, and made my way to Heracles's front door and knocked.

"Fancy seeing you on my doorstep," he teased when he greeted me. "You're usually quite scarce."

"Yeah, the outcast, I know, I know." I rolled my eyes, not having time for the same shit, different day crap.

Heracles shrugged. "We all have a history."

He was right, of course. Every god or goddess had a beef with someone. Or with everyone. It was part and parcel of being immortal. It was hard not to have issues when you were in each other's faces forever. And it got damn boring on Mount Olympus, so many deities created problems for the sake of entertainment.

"How can I help you?" he asked, his hands shoved into the pockets of his cargo pants.

"I'm headed to the Underworld."

He raised his eyebrows before nodding, gesturing for me to come inside. I followed him in and closed the door behind us.

"I didn't think it was quite your vibe," he quipped.

Was that dry humor?

"It's not," I replied. "But I'm pretty sure it's where X is holding Catina. I want to know what the odds are of her still being alive, and you were down there that time to kidnap Hades's hound, Cerberus."

Heracles sighed, his brow furrowing with that worried look he often gave off. I swore, some days I wasn't sure who was the biggest killjoy. Heracles or Poseidon. "Yeah, the twelve labors were a long time ago."

I waited for him to tell me more, waffle on about his heroic deeds. But it sucked when people brought up the past. We'd all had it hard sometimes. Heracles could get over it.

"If X can take souls, I don't see why he can't prevent Catina's from slipping into the stream with the rest of them. From what I've heard, he's looking for trouble with Elyse, so it would make sense. And it's the last place any of you would look." Heracles rubbed a hand over his stubbled jawline.

"Yeah, don't remind me how badly we've failed the last week and a half."

Heracles sat on his coffee table, as if it were a seat. "Look, this isn't my problem, so I'm staying out of this one. Not because I don't care about Elyse, but because it's not in my job description." He sounded so damn bitter. What the fuck was his problem?

"Thanks for that," I said sarcastically.

"But," Heracles continued, pulling a face at me for snapping at him, "I got in there once, and even went on the edges one time with Elyse to help her understand her powers by meeting the Fates. So I'm sure if I could do it, you can pull off some miracle, too."

"Nice of you to believe in me." My response came out a little scornful, but Heracles and I weren't always on the best terms. He was one of the gods who thought I was a coward.

They all did, but I was changing my ways. And soon, Heracles would come to see he'd been a prick for too long.

"Thanks," I said when there was nothing more to say. "I appreciate it."

He nodded, and I let myself out. I had no reason to stick around with Mr. Unhelpful. Besides, I had to get going. Hero's mission and all that.

Going to the Underworld wasn't exactly a party. I shut my eyes and pictured the Underworld, stretching my energy out for the location underground, and my flesh prickled. I opened my eyes to find I'd ended up in a great stone hall I could only describe as the lobby of the dead. It smelled stuffy, like an old trunk that hadn't been opened in a century.

Silvery walls spread behind me while black tiles ran under my feet. An antique gothic lounge sat against the wall, with red velvet fabric and black wooden feet carved in elaborate patterns that resembled oversized paws. It overlooked the River Styx, which stretched out before me.

Charon lounged on an old wooden beach chair near the water, as if he were on a fucking vacation.

"What do you want?" he asked when he saw me.

"What everyone desires when they get here," I stated. "To get to the other side."

He laughed at me. Laughed. As if this were funny.

"Does it look like I'm joking?" I snarled.

Charon snorted loudly. "No. But you immortals always think you can call the shots. If you have your coin and you're dead, I'll take you over. But seeing you're immortal, and you don't actually belong here, you don't get to go."

I started getting pissed off, my pulse racing. He was an arrogant little shit.

"So, you only take dead people over, huh?" I questioned. "What if *you're* dead?"

Charon rolled his eyes. "Seriously? A threat is pathetic. You can't kill me, asshole. Only two people have come across here alive, aside from Hades, Persephone, and X."

"Two?" I asked.

Charon yawned as if he were bored by my company.

"Heracles, way back when. And that little human X dragged with him the other day. He has the ability to take people across the river."

Oh, goodie. We were finally getting somewhere, and I was right about my suspicions.

"Is she still alive?" I coaxed, lowering my voice to attempt to connect to his compassionate side.

Charon kept staring out over the still water. It was so dark, I couldn't see anything beneath its surface. "Not really my problem, is it? Seeing that she's already over there, so even if she's dead, my job's done."

I felt like punching the asshole in the face. He rubbed me the wrong way. That happened when your job was secure—you started being unhelpful.

"Thanks," I said.

Charon whistled, looking out over the river that ran black. I turned around and returned to Earth. I hadn't seen Catina with my own eyes, but I'd found out what I'd gone to the Underworld for. Or at least, I knew that X took Catina there. I still didn't know if she was alive. But Heracles had crossed and survived—and he was half-human—so there was hope yet.

But I had to believe she was alive. If she were dead, this would all be for nothing. And if she hadn't survived, it would hurt like a bitch once Elyse found out.

It would've been better if I had more evidence, but she needed to know what was going on now. I'd want to know if the roles were reversed. And I was a lot of things, but a lying son of a bitch wasn't one them.

When I appeared in Elyse's living room, she hurried from the bedroom. She wore jeans and a tank top, something I didn't see her in often. She was either training, in pajamas, or fighting when I saw her.

"I found her," I declared, my voice booming louder than I expected.

Elyse's eyes widened and she grabbed my hand in hers, squeezing it. "Where?"

"In the Underworld."

I moved closer to Elyse and kissed her cheek. If her mind was whirling right now, I didn't blame her.

Her brows pulled in. "How's that possible?"

"I don't know." I headed to the couch, taking Elyse by her hand, and we sat down. She stayed with me for a moment before jumping up again.

"We have to go get her," she insisted, her shoulders stiff, her hands balled into fists as she paced the room.

I rubbed my hands down my pant legs. "I have to warn you."

She stopped and looked at me, terror in her eyes, and she pressed her fists to her stomach as if she might be sick.

"I couldn't get past the damn ferryman on the River Styx. He told me she's there, but I couldn't see her for myself. I don't know if she's still alive." I held my breath for a second, hating saying those words out loud.

But there it was, straightforward and honest. The truth hurt, but it was better than a lie.

"She has to be alive," Elyse said, nodding her head, her voice trembling. Her determination was admirable, and I agreed with her. It wouldn't make sense if she were dead. But we still didn't know.

"And I'm going to get her," she added.

"You can't die to cross the river," I said. "What if you don't come back?"

"I have one more life."

"Fuck, Elyse!" I cursed angrily. Of course, I'd expected her to pull this stunt. "You can't keep giving your lives away as if they mean nothing. You only have two left. What happens after that, huh?"

"I can't just leave her," Elyse growled, her anger rising to meet my own.

I massaged my temples, trying not to let this turn into a fight when it wasn't necessary. "I didn't say you can't go." Because stopping her was close to impossible. "You just can't go alone."

She thought about it for a moment, her gaze drifting to the ceiling and back on me.

"Fine," she agreed. "Come with me, then."

I nodded. "You know I never back down from a fight."

The rising anger between us evaporated, and it was just us in the room again.

Elyse pressed her hand against her forehead as if she had a headache, her breaths racing. "Can we leave now?"

"We're getting the others together, too. I don't want to chance it with just the two of us."

She rubbed the back of her neck and turned to the window, looking out but not seeing anything.

"What if it's too late? What if waiting any longer will be the difference between her living and dying?

The others will try to stop us, waste time Catina doesn't have."

I knew why she was worried. But I had to keep Elyse alive. We all did.

"Look, X is doing this to look for a fight with you. So we have to make sure when we bring him that fight, we're going to win. He won't let Catina die, or there'll be no reason for you to go. He's going to keep her alive."

"But what if he doesn't and we go anyway because we're hoping?" Her eyes glistened, and she fought that desperation to beg me to let her charge after X, to open the door to the Underworld for her. But for once in my life, I wasn't the one barging into battle without thinking it through and understanding my enemy.

I got that she didn't trust X wouldn't kill her friend. Humans didn't trust each other, and it showed in their history.

"We're going down there, with all of us, and we're going to get Catina out alive. We'll beat X's ass, and we're going to end this once and for all. X wants a fight —we'll give him something he won't forget. There *are* downfalls to being immortal, and he'll find that out."

Elyse sank down into the armchair, exhausted. "Okay," she breathed. "Let's call the troops, then we go after X. I'm not sitting this one out."

X would never give us the human girl if it meant he'd missed out on fighting Elyse. He wanted her and only her. The rest of us were an irritation more than anything else. But Elyse would have four bodyguards to stop X from doing whatever he planned. Because I wasn't losing her for the sake of one human life.

It sounded bad, but if I had to choose between Catina and Elyse, between any of the humans, all of the humans, and Elyse, I knew exactly whom I'd go with.

CHAPTER 16

Poseidon

*A*res had found Catina. My heart beat with excitement knowing we had a location where we could corner the bastard. It was a turn of events that left me as surprised as the rest of the guys. Of all the people who could have found her, Ares wasn't someone I expected to do the job.

But he was starting to step up and prove he was worth his spot on the team, and no matter who found the human girl, we could finally do something to improve the situation.

Although no one knew if she was still alive, except she had to be. X wouldn't have taken her to the Underworld only to kill her. Even if Elyse worried about the possibility. And I didn't blame her. Death trapped her best friend, so of course, anyone would jump to the worst possible conclusion. Including me... but I held out hope that we'd find her alive.

Elyse had gone to the bathroom. Apollo slouched on her sofa, and I stood in front of the television. Not only were the couches too small to sit on—they were human-sized, but they were all big boys, so the seat looked like a toddler's toy with Apollo's ass parked in it.

"What're we going to do to stop her from entering the Underworld?" I asked. "We can't give X what he wants."

"We can't stop her," Apollo responded. "Not unless we trick her somehow. You know how she is, and I'm not going to do that."

I scrubbed a hand over my face. He was right; we couldn't stop her unless we betrayed her. I wasn't willing to do that either, but I worried we were delivering her to X, which was exactly what he wanted.

"What if she gets hurt?" I hesitated.

"We'll have to make sure that doesn't happen," Apollo said. "If we all go, maybe we can make a difference. Remember that time we all stood together when X hounded her? He backed down."

"He did. But he found a better way to get to her. I'm sure this is because of everything that's happened, because of how strong she's become and the fact we're all on her side. He didn't plan for that."

"None of us did."

He was right. We hadn't planned on getting

involved with her fight. Or to fall in love with her. It was why we were all here, ultimately. But now she was in our lives, it was our fight, too.

I bet X was furious about our involvement, and it explained why he'd pulled out all the stops. But he hadn't seen the kind of war a god willingly waged when it came down to love. And Elyse was one-of-a-kind. X had at least three gods on his case with us all fighting for Elyse.

Who knew where Hades stood and where his heart was in all of this. He loved her, but what was he willing to sacrifice? How much was he planning to fight against someone who was essentially part of him? How that worked exactly I wasn't sure, but we'd find out if he came with us.

Then again, he hadn't done anything about X so far.

The bathroom door opened, and Elyse appeared, dressed in her workout gear. She marched into the living room, moving differently, stronger in the way she carried herself. She was lithe, light on her feet, and you only had to look at her once to know she was a warrior. Gone was the scared girl I met when I'd first came to Earth.

Everything had changed now. She became less and less human after her deaths. Which was the only reason I was even remotely okay with taking her with us to the Underworld. Still, my gut twisted that things would go wrong. This was uncharted territory for all of us.

"I know you guys were gossiping about me." Elyse

flopped down next to Apollo, and he wrapped an arm around her back. Even with barely any space left on the loveseat he occupied, he shifted, making room.

"We were just talking about going to the Underworld," Apollo explained smoothly. "You know we worry."

Her cheeks flushed in an adorable way. "I know. But I'll be okay."

"We'll make sure of that." I squared my shoulders.

Easier for all of us. She might have been brought up to battle on her own, but things were different now. To succeed, we'd work as a team.

Apollo glanced at me before speaking. "And you think we're going to sit back while you're in danger? Ain't happening."

Elyse chuckled, clearly happy with Apollo's response, and leaned back against the couch. I couldn't help but slide my gaze over her body. She was beautiful in so many ways. But a fit, fighting body was a delicious thing to behold, and Elyse was as toned and strong as they came.

My dick punched up in my pants, and I squirmed a little. Elyse glanced at me. Something shifted in the atmosphere. I wasn't sure what I felt, but it was powerful and intoxicating, fogging my brain.

I sat in the armchair closest to Elyse. She lifted her body away from the couch as if an invisible force pulled her toward me. And I was drawn to her, too. Whatever was going on, it was like a magnetic lure I didn't want to ignore. Our energies seemed to fluctuate around Elyse, they seemed to fluctuate lately, calm some days, and lustful others. Just like now.

Her power flared, and the room filled with electricity, so thick, I breathed it in when I inhaled. The hairs on my nape lifted.

Apollo moved his hand and put it on her leg. He was aware of the change, too. I'd never felt something like this with any woman I'd been with. Not even with Elyse our first time. This was new, and it reminded me of lust but even more forceful. It was riddled with her power, and mine rose to match. Apollo's magic grew, too. Something had changed between us, and I remembered the shift in the air when we all touched after we comforted Elyse in her apartment.

Despite the seriousness of the situation, I desired her, and my body buzzed with anticipation, as if a switch had been flicked on inside me. I wanted her on her back, naked, fucking hard and fast—now. I swallowed hard and glanced at Apollo. He needed to leave, or maybe he could watch. But when I met his gaze, hunger flooded his eyes. He sensed the same lustful arousal. He tasted the pull the same way I did, and he longed to fuck her just as badly. If Ares was here, he'd wear the same look, but he was out in the city somewhere. Maybe fetching Hades.

"What's happening?" Elyse asked as she licked her lips, staring at both of us like prey.

"I don't know," I admitted, but my breaths raced as my pants tightened from my erection.

Apollo moved his hand up Elyse's leg. She studied his hand before she looked at him, her lips parted.

Whatever happened next, it wouldn't exclude any of us. The energy intensified, and the gods didn't exactly care about shit like privacy.

But Elyse was fine with it too, as she wasn't yelling at us to leave.

I lifted myself out of the armchair, leaned forward, and kissed her. When our lips touched, electricity shot through my body, and I groaned. Elyse responded to the power with a moan of her own. Her hand glided toward Apollo, and I sensed she was touching him. The way he gasped gave enough confirmation.

He dipped his head to her neck while I kissed and nuzzled her. I moved my hand onto her breast. Apollo reached for the other.

Elyse broke the kiss between us and tasted Apollo's mouth. I watched them, saw their lips meld together, as I continued to still massaged her breast, pinching her nipple through her shirt and bra.

I ached for more, so much more. So, I took her hand and pulled her up to stand. I grazed her mouth with mine again, running my touch over her exquisite form. Apollo moved too, standing behind her as his hands joined mine on Elyse.

When I broke the kiss, I pulled her tank top down and licked the soft skin between her breasts. One of her hands was in my hair, the other reaching around to the back of Apollo's neck.

My dick strained against my pants. Hell, they had to go.

Apollo started working her shirt up, and I left a trace of pecks across every bit of skin he exposed. Elyse's breathing grew shallow and erratic, and I inhaled the scent of her arousal. I didn't know how comfortable humans were with things like this, but Elyse was taking it in stride.

Her power rippled over my skin, tugging at my dick, and I groaned. Apollo let out a similar sound. It was almost animalistic. He tugged her top off, and her bra slipped loose. He'd already found the clasp of her sports bra and undone it. I pulled it off and Elyse stood topless in front of me.

Apollo cupped one breast. I sucked Elyse's nipple into my mouth, and she whimpered. Between the two of us, we overwhelmed her with sensation, but I needed more.

Her aura was gleaming with lust. Even if we wanted to stop, we stood no chance.

Apollo spun Elyse so she faced him. He kissed her hard. Her hands moved up and around his neck. I took the time to work her pants over her hips. Apollo and I were still dressed, but she was getting naked, and that was what mattered. When her pants were down, Elyse stepped out of them. I reached for my dick as I took in the sight of her body—her curved ass, those toned legs —and stroked myself.

I pulled off my shirt. I'd had enough of being dressed when she wasn't.

As if Elyse knew what I was doing, she heaved up Apollo's shirt, and he helped her get rid of it.

I rushed out of my pants, and once naked, I stepped closer to Elyse, sandwiching her between Apollo and me. I rubbed my dick against her ass, ran my hands over her back, her breasts, tugging at her nipples.

Apollo took the opportunity to get rid of his pants, too.

When he was naked, Elyse looked down at his hard dick. I couldn't see her face, but I imagined her smiling. Apollo reached around and caressed her ass, pulling her body closer, then spun her around again so that she faced me. One thing I had to say about him—Apollo was great at sharing. And this was a first for me...a threesome, but I wasn't here for Apollo. For Elyse, I'd do anything.

Even though she faced me, Apollo pressed her tightly against his body. He cupped her breast with one hand and reached between her legs with the other. Her eyes rolled back, and she moaned when he pushed his fingers into her slit, finding her clit. For a moment, he made eye contact with me.

If his hands both weren't busy, I'd have given him a high-five.

While he rubbed her pussy, I reached for Elyse's

small hand—her skin was so soft—and placed it on my dick. Her fingers wrapped around my shaft, and I growled when she started pumping up and down.

I leaned forward and sucked her free nipple into my mouth, trying to concentrate while she slid her hand over my cock. I rode a wave of pure bliss, dreaming of a world where Elyse was mine forever.

Apollo let go of her, drifting his hands over her hourglass body. The moment she was free from his grasp, Elyse knelt in front of me, her eyes dark and deep and looking into mine as she took my cock into her mouth.

"Fuck," I breathed.

Elyse bobbed her head back and forth as she licked me, cupping my balls with one hand and drawing me deeper into her mouth. Apollo undid her braid, running his hands through her hair and loosening the strands.

God, we all had a thing for her hair.

"Elyse," I gritted out when she pushed me closer to the edge, to where my heart beat so hard it thrummed, and I was so close to exploding. Of course, I could go on for days if I wanted to; one orgasm wasn't going to stop me. But I'd come in her mouth if she wasn't careful.

She looked up at me and smiled, the generous tile of her mouth almost wicked while continuing without missing a beat. She knew what she was doing and what she wanted. Hell, she was sexy.

My dick jerked in her mouth, and I released, groaning as my balls tightened and she sucked me dry. She swallowed me down, and I wobbled a little unstable on my legs.

When she sat back, her eyes were wide, and she smiled at me.

"I want some of that," Apollo breathed. He sat on the couch, still running his hands through Elyse's hair.

She looked over her shoulder at him before she shifted, positioning herself between his knees. I sank into the armchair and watched as she took Apollo into her mouth and started doing the same thing she'd done to me.

He let out an animalistic growl and buried his hands in her hair, guiding her, pushing her down farther so she took him in deeper and deeper, all the way down her throat, her lips stretched wide.

"Zeus Almighty," Apollo moaned, and he moved his hips, pumping into her mouth as she lowered farther down onto his dick.

She didn't make him orgasm. He didn't allow her to. Before she could get that far, he pushed her back so that his dick slid out of her mouth with a pop. He pulled her up and spun her around, lifting her onto the couch with one arm. She was barely on her back, her legs wide when Apollo plunged into her.

Elyse cried out, and I watched him fuck her. It took me a moment to recover after the orgasm but seeing them together left me ready to roll again almost immediately. I stood. I wanted in on the action.

Apollo stared up at me. He knew what I wanted. We both desired as much as we could get.

He pulled back, and Elyse sighed.

I sat on the couch, and Elyse shifted, climbing onto me. "Hey, sexy," she purred.

Slowly, she sank onto my dick. It disappeared into her wet pussy easily, despite my size, and she started moving her hips, riding me. Her hands pressed on the couch on either side of my head as she braced herself. And her tits bounced.

Apollo towered behind her. He ran his hands over her back, through her hair. His hands went lower down until he was touching her ass. I felt him slide his fingers down, catching some of our juices and spreading them over her ass.

Elyse shivered on top of me, and I held on to her hips, taking over the movement. I wanted her to be still. I bucked my hips and fucked her from beneath.

Apollo remained behind her, and she widened her eyes when he fingered her ass. She looked over her shoulder, and Apollo kissed her, drawing her whimpers into his mouth while I fucked her.

When he pushed his dick into her ass, Elyse let out a cry, and his dick rubbed up against mine, only a membrane separating us. I carried on fucking her and Apollo joined in, moving his dick in and out, finding my rhythm.

Elyse braced herself on the couch as she rode me, crying out with pleasure, my hips lifting beneath her and Apollo fucking her from behind. She screamed out, and we groaned and grunted.

I grew closer to a second orgasm when Elyse came undone. She tightened on top of me and her body clamped down on my bulge, squeezing and sucking my cock. Apollo groaned when she did.

The force that had grown between us strengthened further, somehow increased by our union, the three of us locked together in a way I'd never experienced with anyone. My energy was cold and misty, like a breeze from the ocean. Apollo's was cool and calming. But between us, Elyse's magic was a fiery furnace, ready to consume us all.

Apollo was the first to release. He couldn't hold back any longer, and his dick punched and kicked inside her. My arousal increased until it was almost impossible to bear.

Elyse orgasmed again, and it kickstarted mine, and between the three of us, the sexual intensity and the fire of our magic took our breaths away.

Elyse collapsed on my chest, and Apollo pulled back. Once we no longer supported her between us, she slipped off my lap and lay on the couch, gasping and panting, a pink flush across her body and her sex messy and slick with what we'd done.

Apollo collapsed on the armchair, and we sat together in silence, catching our breath, each of us glowing, smiling.

The lust faded in time, but the fiery power remained in the room, hanging low like fog.

"If this was what three of us are together," Apollo finally spoke, "imagine what we can do when all of us stand together against X."

I rubbed a hand through my hair, unable to stop staring at my Elyse, sitting there all naked and delicious.

"Let's hope it's this intense," Elyse said.

I glanced at Apollo. Did she mean sexually, or regarding the war against X?

But right now, did it matter?

CHAPTER 17

Elyse

*I*f we were going to battle, we'd need all the help we could get. Yes, I was determined to get Catina back, even if it meant traveling to the Underworld. I'd sat back, waiting, for too damn long and now, I needed to kick some serious butt. And after the incredible sexy time I spent with Poseidon and Apollo, the magic between us flaring in a way I'd never felt before, it was better to go as a team than alone. We'd somehow bonded, our energies intensifying, and I didn't care what Poseidon said about being cautious. I'd use whatever arsenal I had access to in order to save my friend. I itched to get started.

But I needed all four gods with me. I had to learn to work as team better. Especially since the guys weren't leaving my side. That was something new for me, but I was open to the challenge. The more, the merrier, right? Besides, this fight wasn't only between X and me anymore. Since he'd escaped, thanks to Hades's poor view of life and love, this fight had become about so much more than saving the humans. Catina. Hades. Myself.

Which was why I wanted Hades with us when we went to the Underworld. The team wouldn't be complete without him—I'd seen how X backed away when the four gods had stood with me, when he sought me out. And seeing the friction between Hades and the other gods, they all agreed it was best if I went to see him on my own.

We needed that unity again.

And I was convinced if I asked Hades to join us, he'd agree. After all, the last two times we'd been together had been very different from our previous meetings. Until recently, Hades's attraction toward me had been purely sexual. A hell of a lot had came down to lust between us whenever we were together, and I'd been convinced for a time that was all there'd been.

But lately, Hades had shown me a vulnerable side of himself. There was so much more affection there than in his closed-off, aggressive side. In a strange way, it excited me to know there was a chance we could be more than just friends with benefits.

That exposed, empathetic side of him was the one I wanted to appeal to now. We needed him to help out and get Catina back. And seeing Hades never meant for anyone to get hurt, much less Catina, my best friend, I was sure he'd be happy to help.

When I knocked on his front door, it took him a while to open up. He looked irritated when he opened the door, his hair scruffy, exhaustion in his eyes, even after he saw me.

"Can we talk?" I asked when he didn't invite me inside. It looked like he was in a bad mood.

"I guess we can." He just stood there, staring out into the distance.

He seemed a little sarcastic, or maybe I was just skeptical—the man I'd seen the last two times was gone, and I'd be lying if I said I wasn't gutted.

"Can I come in?" I pushed again, not nearly as forthcoming as I'd been a moment before. Hades was a son of a bitch. There were no two ways about it.

"Yeah," he finally said, stepping aside. He seemed unhappy with me in his space, but he'd have to suck it up. My expectations for this chat wavered. I didn't get the feeling I'd have as good a conversation with him as I'd imagined. I wasn't sure what was going on, but the Hades I saw now was much more along the lines of the villain I'd thought he was.

"What do you want?" he challenged. He really didn't want me here. What the hell was going on?

"I want to talk to you about Catina. Ares found her in the Underworld. X is keeping her there. We're going to get her, and I wanted to ask if you'll come with us."

"No, thank you," Hades responded without even appearing to think about my question.

"Just like that?" I exclaimed in shock, my stomach twisting. "Don't you care?"

"Not about Catina," Hades declared with zero emotion in his voice. "Why would I? I don't even know her. She's just another inconsequential human."

"That inconsequential human is my best friend," I said tightly. "And you are partly to blame for her disappearance."

Hades barked a sarcastic laugh. "How do you figure that?"

"You're responsible for X's release. He's running around, causing shit all over the place, and you're the one who should be able to rein him in."

Hades narrowed his eyes. I didn't like the way he looked at me as if I was just another one more of his enemies. I thought everything had changed between us; I'd assumed he felt something more for me than the strange rivalry we'd had that was always laced with sex.

"I'm not interested," he replied coldly.

He didn't even offer an explanation, an excuse, anything. I stared at him for a moment, surprised he was so extremely closed off to me. Much more than before even.

"If I didn't know better, I'd think you didn't even care about me," I said softly.

"You see, this is how everyone pisses me off." The bitterness in his voice was out of place and caught me off-guard. "Everyone seems to think there's no other way than to love. But I'm not interested in love, sweetheart. Not anymore. I'm sorry you thought it was something that could happen, but I don't love." He almost growled the words, and I trembled at the anger he spewed toward me.

A fiery rage slingshotted through me, and a blaze crawled up my spine and over my head. Why was he messing with me like this? What about the last two times we'd been together? I didn't understand why he bothered showing me that side of him if he was only going to cut me out again.

"Was I just a convenience while you were feeling weak?" I let my anger show and lifted my chin to make myself look bigger.

"Don't flatter yourself. I was bored."

"And now I'm the pathetic one who thought I could be anything more to you than sex." My words shook from pure rage, shielding the shredding of my heart.

Hades's shrugged response only made it worse.

I groaned, exasperated. I was so over his shit, over how he blew hot and cold, over how he could be incredibly attractive one moment and revolting the next. I was sick and tired of fighting the monster he'd set free, whether he'd willed it to be or not. I was tired of being scared, tired of being angry, tired of being tired. Who the fuck did he think he was to treat me this way? And I hated that I let him hurt me, and I felt sick to my stomach that I cared, that my throat thickened with the tears pricking my eyes from him pushing me away.

"You know what?" I snapped, my hands curling into fists. "I've just about had it with you and all the time you've wasted."

Before he could respond, I launched toward him and punched him in the face. Our fights always turned physical—he was the only guy who didn't pull his punches because I was a woman. He saw me as a worthy adversary. He fought me with all his power, as if he knew I could take it.

And I could. Now more than ever.

His mouth dropped open—clear surprise at my attack—but he retaliated a moment later. He wasn't one to stand on ceremony, and he placed a kick in my gut. I'd already anticipated it and started moving away, so it wasn't nearly as effective as he intended. With the barrier broken, the fight had started, and we both lunged into it with everything we had.

My power surged through me, heightening and expanding around us, the heat building. The energy I'd been practicing using lately was scorching hot. The type of heat that could melt metal. But Hades's ability had been fiery all along. I remembered one of the first times I sensed it, how I'd felt him burning me up inside.

Of course, we'd been fucking then. Now we were fighting—again. It was always one or the other with him, and I'd been a fool to think our relationship could be anything else. Ha, no...not relationship. Just a fucked-up mess.

"You're strong," Hades growled while we punched and kicked and spun around, evading each other, attacking when we thought we could get through. "Stronger and faster than before. But you'll never win going up against a god. Not against me, and I doubt you'll ever win against X."

"If you don't want to be on my side, fine," I seethed, breathing hard. I elbowed him on the jaw, and he staggered backward. He recovered almost immediately and counter-attacked. "But I didn't think you'd be against me."

"I'm against everyone. The world isn't a welcoming place, and I don't expect anyone to back me up."

"Yeah, your skepticism is clear. It's a pity you seem to think everyone is against you when there are people out there who care for you."

"If you say Persephone, I'm going to gag," Hades spat. "She cares, but she couldn't even love me."

"I was talking about me," I yelled, ducking a punch. I retaliated, and he managed to sidestep me, staying out of the way.

He began to laugh, and the sound grated on my nerves. It was sarcastic, mocking. Hades was taking my affection for him as a joke. It only irritated me more—I wouldn't have invested any kind of affection in him if he hadn't shown me his softer side. But maybe I'd been wrong about him. Maybe he was playing me, bored, as he said.

"You really are a dick." I kicked him in his sternum.

He only took one step back, smirking. "Finally you notice."

The sound of menacing laughter had us both spinning. X himself leaned against the wall not far from the kitchen entrance, his arms crossed over his chest as he watched us battle.

"The two of you are like an old married couple," he mocked. His voice danced around me, brushing against my skin and making me shiver. But my anger was greater than my fear at this point. I breathed heavily, my heart pounding, and I was ready to launch at X, but Hades stepped between us and with a well-aimed punch, he flattened me.

I looked at him from the floor. He towered above me, a smug smile on his face.

"Thanks," I said sarcastically. "Not only are you not willing to help me, but you're also planning on getting in my way. It just gets better and better."

Hades ran a hand down his face and sat on the couch. He couldn't hide his heavy breathing, but other than that, it didn't look like my attack had affected to him.

X still leaned against the wall, looking nonchalant as fuck, and I had a feeling no matter what I did, asking for Hades's help wasn't going to work. Plus, X wasn't here to fight, only to spectate. To laugh at me, and on my own, I couldn't take him down. I climbed to my feet, rubbing my jaw, which ached from Hades's hit.

"You know this is a bad sign," I said to Hades, pointing at X. "He's only here because you refuse to accept the good side of yourself. I'm sure you've figured that out by now."

Hades's face tightened. If he already knew, he seemed to have accepted that fact. If he hadn't known yet, he didn't seem to care.

"It's every man for himself, sugar," he sneered. "I'm not going to fuss about everyone else who needs saving. There are enough of you in the world willing to do that."

I wanted to attack him again, drive my fist into his face. He knew just which buttons to push. But I held back, clenching my jaw. It wouldn't make a difference —I'd never win a fight against Hades. And he didn't have a limit to what he was willing to do to me.

That asshole had killed me before. Sure, I accepted he'd done it to save me, but now I doubted his reasoning.

So instead of engaging with X, or continuing the fight with Hades, I turned around and stormed to the front door. X wasn't here to battle me because it wasn't a big enough audience. Fucking bastard. I hated how everything reduced to dramatic value for these gods… even killing someone.

"Don't think this is going to stop me from getting her back," I snarled to X, my hand already on the doorknob. I looked at Hades. "As for you, I think I'm just about done."

I couldn't read the look that crossed his face—something that seemed a lot more emotionally charged than I expected. But I wasn't going to read too much into it. Hades had shown me his true colors. I thought I could lean on him, and he'd proven he wasn't someone who'd ever have my back.

That Hades had some kind of heart was nothing more than a myth.

CHAPTER 18

Hades

I was in a shitty mood, and my adrenaline was on a rampage. X's appearance hadn't improved my confrontation with Elyse. I struggled to control myself around her as it was, and as much as I *had* tried to be the nice guy and give her what she wanted, fear and reality seared through me. Even more so after seeing Persephone. That night we visited the Grand Canyon, I'd realized I was falling for Elyse so fucking hard, but what then? Get my heart smashed all over again, become a laughing stock? I couldn't go through that again, not after all the shit I faced with Persephone. Every time I considered letting myself go there with Elyse, terror spiked through my chest, reminding me of what awaited me when I failed. Because I always failed.

I swallowed the thickness in my throat, my heart racing, still remembering Elyse's exquisite smile and her laughter when we chatted over the various meanings of the constellations. Those were moments I needed to forget and stop torturing myself. Especially when I had X to do that for me.

It never put me in a good mood to see him, but lately, X and I just weren't on the same page anymore.

That was saying something for the God of the Underworld and the Greek Grim Reaper.

"What the fuck are you doing here?" I barked at him after Elyse had stormed out. I was shaking with fury that he'd driven her away.

Sure, I was the one who'd made her angry. I'd refused to help her. Maybe I shouldn't have done that. But I was terrified of what I was feeling for her. It pissed me off that I couldn't control my affections. After I lost Persephone, after I'd realized the whole thing had been one big joke, I'd promised myself to never love again. Then Elyse came into my world and tore at my heart. It fucking scared me.

If my brothers and sisters were right, love was something I was incapable of anyway.

But with Elyse, our relationship was something else. I couldn't help how I felt about her, and not being able to deal with such confusion only made me furious.

"I had a feeling you were stirring up problems, and I wanted to watch." X's razor-sharp teeth were on display through his toothy grin.

He pushed away from the wall and seemed to float toward me. I remained seated on the couch, my legs wide, leaning back as if I didn't care he was in my space. If I showed him he irritated me, he'd only make it worse. X was nothing but a deadly pain in the ass.

"I wasn't stirring up problems." I shouldn't have had to defend myself, but I didn't want to admit I'd driven Elyse away. Even though I had. Admitting you were wrong was a bitch.

"Yeah, it looked like she got upset for no reason at all." Mirth danced behind his words. He dropped into one of my armchairs, and I hated that he made himself at home in my space. But X was part of me, and I suppose I should've expected it.

"Look, if you're not here for any good reason, then kindly fuck off," I said.

X laughed. His teeth were very sharp up close, the fangs of a monster. But nearly everything else about him looked human now. The more souls he consumed, the more human he became. It was almost as if he'd be able to kill more people now, purely because he looked like they'd trust him. He was in predator mode.

Almost.

When X first arrived on Earth, he'd looked like a kind of daemon, the way humans describe them. He was much stronger now, but he looked more trustworthy. It was a deadly combination.

And it wasn't like I didn't want to help Elyse get her

friend back. I wanted her to be happy. I cared about her, even though I'd said I didn't.

But I couldn't get involved without losing a piece of myself. If I acknowledged how I felt about her, I'd end up getting hurt again. And I didn't like getting hurt. Too much had happened in my life for me to accept anymore.

"Well, if you're not going to fight her, I will," X growled.

"I thought you didn't come for that." I sat forward on the couch.

X pulled up his shoulders and stirred, stretching like a feral animal "Yeah, well, we can all do with a little bit of fun."

Before I could answer him, he disappeared. He was going after Elyse. I might have told her I didn't care, that I wasn't interested, but I wasn't going to let X take her. She couldn't be very far away. He was going to cut her off and fight her.

And I had to be there to look after her. My pulse was on fire, and I shot to my feet.

Even as I rolled my eyes at myself, irritated I couldn't just let Fate do what it wanted with her. I disappeared into a scramble of magic.

It wasn't hard to track down Elyse. Her power signature rippled in the air, and she stood in the middle of a cloud of darkness. X had already found her. My heart thundered with urgency to shield her.

When I took form, I found them fighting in an

empty park in a shady part of town where there were boarded-up houses. None of the other guys had showed up yet, so either they were out of range or X somehow blocked them.

Elyse had gotten hold of her scythe—she must have had it in her car. She wielded the weapon against X in a way I hadn't seen her do before. When I saw her at the training center, she'd only been practicing. But this... this was war.

I sensed her anger—her fury at me for not being willing to help her, her rage at X for taking Catina, her loathing at herself for not being able to stop him. My heart went out to her. I hated that I was responsible for this mess. And I wasn't trying to do something about it, either.

I really was an asshole.

I leaped into the fight, helping her against X. Because as strong as she was, and as determined she was, she was still mortal and X was almost a god, like me.

"What are you doing here?" she snarled when I appeared beside her. We fought side by side, but we weren't in unity. "Change your mind? Bored again?"

X started using a lot more power behind his hits, and Elyse was driven back, her expression fierce. She wasn't giving up, and she carried a lot of her own energy, but she wasn't used to fighting with her magic. This was where I came in—manipulating magic was like breathing for a god. Perhaps it was a crutch since we wouldn't have been able to live without it.

"I'm here to help you," I declared.

"Bullshit. You only ever help yourself. What will you gain from this?"

"Believe it or not, I don't want you hurt." I pushed X away with my magic, throwing as much force into him as I could. My skin buzzed as my attack shot out from my hands.

But he didn't stumble backward. He was immune to me—he was a part of me, after all.

He laughed, blowing out a long breath that rattled his lips. "Look at you, trying to be the hero. Had to save your little damsel in distress?"

X threw another fiery ball at me that did the same to me as my power did to him. It was like fighting against myself. Except I wasn't a murderer. All I wanted was to live in peace for a little while, to forget what everyone had done to me. I'd been ignoring it for so long, hoping, praying to be left alone. But it looked like that just wasn't going to happen.

"I'm sick and tired of not knowing who you are," Elyse shouted. The fight increased in intensity, the power so strong, she was starting to buckle under it, driven backward. Her arms trembled, but the fire in her eyes blazed, willing her to keep going. "Why can't you just decide if you want me or not and stick with it?"

I couldn't answer. But even if I could, X didn't give

me a chance. Instead, he moved in a flash and snatched Elyse's arm, then disappeared with her.

"Fuck!" No way would I let her suffer the same fate as her human friend. But X had something else in mind for her, didn't he? After all, he wanted to kill her so she wouldn't be a problem for him anymore. It didn't take a lot for me to understand his thinking. It made sense —in an alternate reality, that was what I'd do, too.

I followed the darkness, moving through the air in a flow of magic that prickled down my flesh, until we took form again at the top of a building in downtown Chicago. For some reason, X had taken us far away from my place, the quiet neighborhood where I'd decided to hole up.

And I knew exactly why.

Here in the middle of the city, even though it was nighttime, many more humans could get hurt. Even if X didn't consume them, Death drove him. It didn't matter how he killed them; he'd make sure he took down the whole building and destroyed a lot more than just Elyse.

"You're so fucking predictable," I shouted at X. He was trying to fight Elyse, but he spun around when he heard me. "You're not going to get away with this. I won't allow it."

He laughed and lunged at me. "Don't be ridiculous," he hissed. "You couldn't stop me even if you tried. I'm part of you. Doesn't it scare you, knowing you have this in you? That this death is really a part of you?"

He attacked me, and we fought, our magic pressing up against each other, our power battling it out all around us while we punched and kicked.

With a cry, Elyse jumped into the battle, too. Her scythe sang as it lashed through the air and the sharp edge connected with X's back. It wasn't as though she could kill him, but he definitely felt pain, and he cried out with a screech nothing short of demonic. He turned on her and unleashed his darkness, wrapping it around her, using it to suffocate her like a straitjacket.

Her eyes rolled in their sockets, and she gasped for air she wouldn't get. Panic latched on to my chest, squeezing me. X was going to kill her, and even if she bounced back, it would be the last death she could recover from. That was his plan.

I couldn't let it happen and cracked my knuckles.

"No!" I cried out. "This isn't part of me." I attacked X, and we fought each other. Our power flared, growing around us. We shrouded the top of the building in darkness and energy. A storm of Underworld magic.

"Get out of here!" I shouted to Elyse, wherever she was. "He's going to kill you!"

X chuckled, the sound forced and bitter. "Too late, little Hades. You think you can stop this, but you can't. When you drew the short straw, this became your inheritance, your legacy. Nothing follows you around but death."

Then, suddenly, X was gone. He disappeared, and I was alone on top of the building. I looked around.

"Elyse!" I called, frantic. She wasn't here, and she was supposed to be standing on the rooftop. I'd told her to leave, but she was a human and she would've used the stairs. And that door remained shut.

When I couldn't see her, my stomach dropped. She could only be in one place. I ran to the edge of the building and looked down. The street was horribly far away, since this building was tall. I ran around, looking on each side. On the third side, I saw her, and my blood ran cold.

She lay at the bottom of the building, her legs twisted at unnatural angles. People scrambled on the street. They must have seen her fall.

I disappeared and reappeared at her side, not caring who saw me. Blood seeped from a crack in her head, ran out of her nose and ears, and her lifeless eyes stared into the distance. I grabbed her lifeless body and let out a cry that had everyone in the street looking at me in shock. Grief expelled with every breath, smothering me, clawing at my heart. Time stood still, and icy tendrils embraced me.

I told her I wouldn't help her, but I never wanted this for her. I'd tried to stop X, but somehow she still died. I hadn't been the one who'd killed her—I'd kept him busy. Elyse must have tripped and fallen off the edge, unable to see with all the darkness cloaking her.

After everything she'd been through, this was

almost ironic. I'd killed her before, then she'd taken her own life, but in the end, her third death—the last she could recover from—had been a pure accident. Though I still blamed the fuckhead X because she wouldn't have been in danger if not for him.

CHAPTER 19

Elyse

*D*arkness shrouded me, leaving me unable to hear or see a thing. The silence deafened me. And I struggled to breathe. It was almost as if the blackness around me was a cloud and breathing through the humidity was impossible.

Where was I? Why couldn't I find myself? I wasn't in my body because I'd died. I had no idea how I knew these things, but something about me felt ridiculously detached. I wasn't ready to go through to my final resting place or be dragged down to the Underworld like the rest of the humans.

But for some reason, I couldn't go home, either.

"Hello?" I called into the abyss.

No reply. The emptiness around me seemed so vast,

and it echoed with my loneliness. I couldn't find anyone, and there was no one here to help me, no one to reach out to, no one to bring me back. This shouldn't have happened—I still had one more life. I should've been able to wake up.

How had I died, anyway? I couldn't remember anything or anyone. But a terrible darkness pressed in on me and kept me isolated from everything that should have anchored me.

I closed my eyes and tried to focus on who I was. Elyse Lowe. Descendant of the Lowe family. Protector of the humans. Zeus's power ran through my veins. And it was for this reason I couldn't die. Not yet. I still had business to take care of. My story wasn't finished.

As if this affirmation was all I'd needed, I started floating. I drifted through the darkness, up, up, up.

When I opened my eyes, I gasped for breath, as if I'd been drowning. I sat up on the bed and groaned, feeling as if I'd been hit by a bus. Everything ached, and a terrible headache thrummed through my skull. But when I inspected my body, there wasn't a mark in sight. No bruises, no blood, aside from some on the clothes I still wore.

So why did it hurt so much? Before, the pain had been gone completely. The other two times I died, I'd woken up perfectly restored.

I lay back onto the comfort of my bed, cocooned by the blanket, and closed my eyes. Now I was conscious again, I remembered everything from my last death. Hades had fought X, stepping in so he wouldn't kill me. The darkness had been too much, a thick cloud of black fog that wrapped around me and wouldn't let go. I'd whirled around, trying to shake it off. It had suffocated me, and I hadn't been able to breathe.

And the next moment, I only knew the sensation of falling, the wind whistling past my ears.

And then, nothing.

While I lay on the bed, the aches in my body started to fade away. It was almost as if my body was slow on the uptake, trying to figure out what was going on after I'd woken up again from being dead. It took a while, but eventually I stopped hurting. I felt stiff and tender, but I wasn't sore. Still, I'd lost my last extra life, and that reality chilled me. When I died next time, there was no coming back. I'd either join the other souls or vanish from existence if X got his claws into me. And it terrified me to know how close I stood to losing everything, but I refused to let fear exist in my mind. Not when I had X to defeat and Catina to save. Those were my priorities.

I pushed myself up on the bed, sitting again.

"Hello?" I called out, the same way I had in the darkness. I expected an answer. Every time I'd died before, someone had been here.

But this time, there was no answer. I was completely alone.

I didn't even know who'd brought me home. Hades? It was almost too much to expect from him. He'd made it very clear he didn't care. I wasn't sure why he'd then attempted to save me, but I wasn't taking it as something I could hold on to.

In a lot of ways, Hades had betrayed me. Even though this time, it was X's fault that I'd died. Indirectly or not, the bastard got what he wanted.

I slid off the bed, stiffly staggered to the bathroom, and splashed water on my face. I studied myself in the mirror. The reflection of myself showed me looking hollowed out, as if I hadn't eaten for a couple of days. Dark circles sat under my eyes. Maybe I hadn't slept, either.

Did being dead count?

What day was it? How long had I been out for? I headed to the bedroom and looked for my phone, finding it on the carpet near the door. Whoever brought me back must have dropped it on the way in. I picked it up, and the battery was dead.

After putting it on charge, I sat down on the bed again, overwhelmed by another wave of darkness. The power was strong this time, death's call so loud that for a moment, I couldn't hear anything else. It was as if I was back in that strange limbo, with nothing but darkness to keep me company. Was this how my dad felt during his last life? He'd once mentioned something to me about feeling like he was drowning all the time, and now I understood what he'd meant. The sensation crashed through me like waves, engulfing me, pulling me under.

I scrubbed my face with my hands and shook my head, trying to get rid of the feeling. Instead, I dug deep for my power to push the new energy away, but just as with any other time I'd died, the power felt unstable, fluctuating.

It would take a while before I figured out how to use it. This was the part I hated most about dying. You know, aside from actually dying.

What bothered me most was that the darkness grew worse each time. I was terrified of what would come next. Would I drown in darkness for eternity? I shivered, unable to shake off the tendrils of death that still clung to me.

What if I didn't want to do this anymore? What if I was tired of battling the inner energy? I couldn't die another time without it being final. If X found me again, if anything went wrong this time, it was the end of the line for me. My hands trembled at my sides, and sweat drenched my skin. My awareness grew that I'd been a fool to sacrifice one of my lives when X confronted me in this bedroom before. Now, with no more lives left, I worried. I should've thought it through. Should've considered what it meant.

But I'd been thinking as a warrior, focusing on quick survival. I'd only thought about the here and now, not about the complete war.

And now it was too late.

When my phone had charged a little bit, I switched it on, waited for it to boot up, and looked at the date. It was Sunday—only one day after I'd died. I'd woken earlier than in the previous deaths…was that why I felt so exhausted? Why hadn't anyone been here when I woke up. Did no one know? Were they all out of town searching for X?

But it had only been one day, and I spent longer than that on my own without my men, so they probably didn't know any different. The first time I died, it was in front of Hades and Apollo, so they took care of me. The second time, Oliver who found me, called Heracles to tell him of my death. And this time, it was only Hades who'd brought me home. Plus, the gods didn't actually sense my deaths, but they should have picked up on my battle with X, yet none of them came.

Thinking back to the battle on the rooftop, I was caught in X's darkness, and I'd never felt so isolated from the world. Could his power have lacerated my connection to the gods? They'd always sensed me fighting him in the past. I couldn't understand their absence.

But Hades had known. And he hadn't bothered to stay with me. Maybe he hadn't told anyone else, either. While anger ought to have boiled deep inside me, I felt something else. A sorrow that I'd been right about Hades. Especially after getting my hopes up when he showed me a vulnerable side of himself. A softer side. The only fool then had been me.

His behavior just confirmed what I'd thought for a while now. Hades only looked out for himself. He was selfish and unkind, a son of a bitch who should go back to the Underworld where he'd come from.

Even if he wasn't the one who set X free, I understood his horrible view of love had caused something like this. But that didn't give him the right to act the way he did. It didn't allow him to do whatever he wanted without consequences.

Hades had chosen to let his past to define him. It was such a stupid, human sentiment. It shouldn't have been something an immortal god would do.

But there it was. Hades was self-centered, and he hadn't learned.

A sudden wave of exhaustion washed over me, and I lay back down on my bed. The fact I was struggling so much after waking up bothered me. My body should've recovered by now, flooding me with energy.

Instead, I lay there, contemplating giving up the fight. Exhausted by battling against everything and everyone.

When I closed my eyes, Catina's face flashed in front of me. Oh, God. How was I meant to save her? How was I going to enter the Underworld and bring her back when I'd be dead for good if I died again? X might not have been the one to kill me this time, but he'd still achieved what he wanted—I was down to my final breath.

And I was fucking terrified of that. Scared if I went

down to rescue Catina, I'd fail again. What if she died? What if I died? I didn't know how I was going to do this now.

Before I died this time, I'd been so damn confident I'd would enter the Underworld and find Catina. Now, going at all—even if I had a team of three or even four gods—seemed like the most foolish thing in the world.

I couldn't go to the Underworld to get Catina. And she was counting on me, waiting for me to rescue her. But so was X.

After dying, I should've been even more powerful. If I practiced for a while, I would be. But right now, my magic was unstable and out of control and out of my grasp. I wasn't going to be able to fight X, no matter where we wound up battling or what the circumstances were. He must have known something like this would happen, that he was buying himself time by forcing my third death on me.

I hated that we'd somehow played right into his hands, given him the upper hand, even.

But whatever his ploy, whatever the reason for my weakness, I couldn't do it. Going to the Underworld wouldn't end well. Not even with the other gods.

Fuck!

I couldn't save Catina. My best friend caught up in this mess because of me.

And after a while, X would tire of entertaining a human and keeping her alive in a place where only dead souls belonged. She was waiting for someone to rescue her and it would never happen. And then, eventually, she'd die. And there was nothing I could do about it.

This was the end of the line for my friend.

I rolled onto my side and closed my eyes, curling my knees up to my stomach, feeling hollow. An empty shell with nothing to offer. Every emotion pushed out from my body. Where I once had hope and light and drive, now only emptiness lay. The urge to cry came and went, hot tears spilling down my cheeks. I took a deep breath and let it out slowly, focusing on every muscle group, forcing myself to relax bit by bit. Slowly, sleep crept up on me, and the darkness that clung to me didn't scare me as much anymore. All I wanted was sleep, to run away from this mess, to escape from the life I'd chosen for myself.

Oh, how I wished I hadn't chosen to follow in my father's footsteps. How I wished I'd chosen to be one of the Lowe family members who forfeited their power, gave up who they were completely. I'd always thought they were a waste of space since they turned their backs on their calling to do something so much bigger. But right now, I envied them. They all lived simple lives, with taxes and relationships being their biggest worries.

If I were transported into a new life where I didn't know any of the gods, and I didn't have to deal with any of these difficulties, I wasn't so sure I'd be upset about it. Except, thinking about the men in my life, I changed my mind. I'd lose them, and I couldn't bear such an existence.

So how was I going to manage this?

I wasn't.

CHAPTER 20

Apollo

A loud knock reverberated through my skull, calling to me, waking me, but darkness cloaked my vision. Where was I?

The banging continued. Louder and louder, and with each passing moment, the panic coiling around my chest tightened.

I searched deep within me and drew on my power, unleashing the brightest light inside, the magic crawling down my arms. In a heartbeat, the shadows around me dissolved, and I stared up at the white ceiling as I lay on the floor behind my couch.

What the fuck? I hadn't been drinking, and the last thing I remembered was coming home for a shower before I visited Elyse.

I got to my feet, fists clenched, and scanned my living room. No one there. Had I passed out?

Another round of knocking, and it came from my front door.

I scratched my head and crossed the room before opening it.

Hades stood there. He hadn't just materialized inside my place, but maybe that was a good thing. I wouldn't have asked questions if he had; I would have simply knocked his block off when I woke up from whatever nightmare I'd had, assuming he was to blame.

He wasn't my favorite person right now. Elyse told me what Persephone had told her. But I didn't care—he was a dick, and I didn't like him. The rest of us were teaming up together to help Elyse take on X, but Hades was too fucking selfish to do anything other than watch out for himself.

Sure, the guy had gone through some stupid heartache. But we'd all had our hearts broken. Some of us more than others. And you didn't see us doing stupid things, did you? Everyone else seemed to be managing their difficulties and ugly pasts in a healthy way.

But Hades had to be the one looking for attention by acting out. He was like a millennia-old child.

"What?" I snapped when he gave me a sheepish look from the doorstep. "I can't imagine you're here for a friendly little visit."

He breathed deeply. "I thought I'd let you know that Elyse died."

"What?" I asked, my tone of voice very different this time, and ice pierced my chest. I didn't feel her fighting X. "Are you fucking with me?"

Hades shook his head. "Believe what you like about me, but I thought I'd tell you."

I grabbed him by the throat. "What game are you playing?"

He smiled at me, despite my death grip. Of course, I couldn't do him any real harm. But, by Zeus, I wanted to.

"What happened?" I inquired when Hades didn't answer me. I still held his neck, even though I couldn't hurt him. And Hades didn't struggle too much to escape from my grip.

"It was an accident, indirectly caused by X attacking her, believe it or not," he choked out. "But no matter how it happened, this was her second-to-last death. You know what it means."

I let go but not without shoving him backward. "Of course I know what it means," I snapped. "When? Where is she?"

"Oh, yesterday. I spend most of Sunday, all night, and this morning by her side. She's probably still out as it should take her a few days to wake up," he said. "So, I wanted to let you know since you'll probably want to be with her. Especially considering none of you seemed to come to her rescue when she fought X." He snarled the words.

"Wait! Isn't today Sunday?" I asked. "And are you blaming this on me?"

He glared at me as if I were an idiot, his brows raising, his head tilted slightly. "It's Monday."

I ran a hand down my face, convinced it was just Sunday. I remembered waking up cloaked in darkness. But I'd lost a full day and hadn't sensed Elyse fighting with X. I always did in the past.

"Fuck!" I gave Hades a fast run down of my guesstimation. "That asshole trapped me so I couldn't help Elyse. Want to the bet he did the same to Poseidon and Ares? Of course, he didn't touch you, because he's part of you." My voice darkened, and my nails bit into my palms as I curled my hands into fists because I was going to kill X.

Elyse had been dead since yesterday, and none of us knew about it and we couldn't help her. Anger very quickly replaced my shock, and my fist shot out, landing on Hades's jaw.

"You released X, and now he's going to kill Elyse."

His head jerked to the side, but he turned his face to me again almost immediately—as if he wanted me to do it again, like he was daring me to do more. But I wasn't in the mood to fight him. If I could kill him, I probably would have.

"Get the fuck out of my house," I hissed through gritted teeth, not knowing what else to say to him. I had to go see her. I was pissed he didn't seek us out earlier, but in the back of my mind, I reminded myself Hades probably used the time with her to grieve, to have alone time with Elyse while she recovered. The thought didn't ease the burning fire in my chest.

He lowered his gaze and sauntered out of my house as if nothing was wrong. As if nothing had ever been wrong. The son of a bitch had to stay out of my way if he wanted me to be civil toward him at all. Because there was no way I'd able to hold back a second time. Sure, he cared for Elyse, but it pissed me off that he acted so nonchalant when Elyse's life was in peril. And he should make it his mission to eradicate X but didn't.

I left the house immediately after Hades did and transported to Elyse's place. As soon as I knew she was all right, I'd check in on Ares and Poseidon.

Heracles arrived at the same time as me.

"Elyse died," I said.

He nodded.

"How did you know?" I asked.

"I was visiting Zeus. He told me. So, I came straight here to check on her."

I told him about X trapping me and the other two. But I was furious as to why the fuck Heracles hadn't told any of us about Elyse right away either. A burning blaze tore through me. Together, Heracles and I hurried toward Elyse's front door. We didn't bother knocking; we just reappeared inside.

Elyse wasn't in the living room. Heracles rushed to

the bedroom with me on his heels. Elyse lay on her bed sleeping. She wasn't dead anymore; she was breathing.

"She's awake already." Heracles pointed out the obvious. "Zeus said the third death would bring her back fast, but this is incredible."

"Nice to know it's entertaining you." I sat on the edge of the bed and ran my fingers through her hair, not caring how long it took her to reawaken, just that she was alive. The strands were still matted with blood. I didn't even want to think about how she'd died. It looked as if it'd been painful.

"Hey, Elyse," I said softly.

Her eyes rolled behind her eyelids, and her face looked younger in a way, but she didn't wake up yet. I went on stroking her hair, gently nudging her until her eyes fluttered open. She looked as if she didn't want to come back to reality.

"Are you okay, sweetheart?" I asked, my heart aching at finding her in this state.

She looked from me to Heracles. "Where were you?" she croaked.

"I came here as soon as I heard about your death from my father. Apollo didn't know," Heracles explained.

"Hades just told me," I added.

Elyse touched her temple while closing her eyes for a brief moment.

"Do you want to talk about it?" I probed.

Elyse looked at me, and her voice wavered. "Oh, Apollo," she whispered, and her eyes filled with tears.

In all the time I'd known her, I couldn't remember ever seeing her so lost. I collected her in my arms and held her against me while she fell apart. She'd always been incredibly strong, but today she was still just a human. And she'd been through so much. Not just for the sake of the other humans, but in part for all our sakes as well.

Heracles came closer and hugged Elyse also. I let her go long enough for him to embrace and hold her. He'd trained her from a young age and watching her in such pain, losing life after life, would have to be difficult.

"You're going to be okay," he said. Then he looked at me. "Take care of her. I need to go talk to our dad again."

My mouth opened to ask him what he was seeing Zeus about, and if it was related to the shitstorm X was causing, but he'd disappeared. Elyse curled her body against mine again, shuddering. I held her as she cried, trying to shake everything that had happened.

"I don't know how I'm going to do this anymore," she finally admitted, her voice thick with tears. "I don't think I'm the right person for the job. Zeus chose wrong."

I shook my head. "Zeus doesn't make mistakes," I reminded her. "And I'm sure after Heracles goes to speak to him, he'll come back and tell you the same thing. You're a warrior, stronger than anyone I've ever seen before. And that includes us immortals."

She kept her head against my chest. She didn't believe me. And I understood why. She'd been to hell and back three times already.

"How am I going to save her?" Elyse wondered, and she was talking about Catina. X still had the human girl. He'd taunted Elyse, and the fucker needed to be stopped.

"We'll do it together," I said, holding her tight, wanting more than anything to scoop her into my arms and take her to a place no one could find her again. A place I knew didn't exist, but if it did, I'd whisk her away in a heartbeat. She didn't deserve everything happening to her.

"I don't think I can go with you to the Underworld," Elyse confided. "There's just so much darkness, and I can't get away from it anymore. It's inside my head, in me. I'm scared it's going to pull me under and not let me go."

I caught a tear rolling over her chin. "Do you know what brings you back every time?"

Elyse lifted a tear-stained face to me and shook her head.

"It's the power of Zeus inside your veins," I explained. "That's what keeps dragging you back from the darkness, from the edge of death. I know you've gone through all the deaths you can recover from, but that doesn't mean Zeus's power isn't in your veins anymore."

She nodded and tucked herself against my chest once again. Maybe this was exactly what she'd needed to hear. Reassurance that all wasn't lost yet.

"I just don't think I'm the person to help her," she mumbled, even though she'd agreed.

"This isn't just about Catina," I added. "She's the embodiment of the people you're supposed to protect. See this as symbolic. If you can save Catina, one person, you can save them all."

"I wish I believed that." Elyse huffed as she pulled away and lowered her gaze from mine.

"You don't have to," I said gently. "Not yet. But you should know, I believe in you. I know you're stronger than anything out there. The reason why X is doing all these things to you is because he knows he can't beat you. He's terrified he might never be able to. He's pulling out all the stops, and it tells me he's scared." And I believed that without a doubt. Why else would he taunt her, kidnap her friend, and stop three gods from getting in the way? If he viewed Elyse as a normal mortal, he'd have killed her right away and been done with it, rather than playing these games. He saw her as an adversary who stood in his way, who could take him down, who was capable of so much more greatness than him. She needed to see for herself.

"What's he afraid of?" she asked.

"Of you. And you owe it to yourself to prove him

right. Show him and the rest of the world who you really are. You are Elyse Lowe, the woman who held out, the woman who, against all odds, carried her legacy for us. And no matter what, I know you'll make it. When I look at you, I see you beaming as bright as the sun. You will shine in victory and light will always follow, all else paling in comparison. I believe in you, Elyse."

She didn't respond at first, but she lay against me, her body warm and small and so fragile, but that was an illusion. A warrior lay inside her. Eventually, she pulled away, sitting up. She met my gaze as she wiped her eyes, and a new expression slid over her features. Gone was the girl needing rescue. Before me was the Elyse I'd first met—fiery, powerful, and determined. She was ready for war.

"Okay," she finally conceded.

"Okay?" I asked, uncertain what decision she'd finally come to.

Elyse sighed. "Okay, I'll try one more time."

I smiled, leaned forward, and pressed my lips against hers. "That's my girl."

CHAPTER 21

Poseidon

*W*hen Apollo told me Elyse had died again, I grew furious, shaking with rage and needing to punch someone. I'd woken up in my backyard, frozen in time by X, just as Apollo and Ares had been. The bastard got us out of the way so he could take her out. We hadn't expected him, but next time, we'd be ready.

Hades hadn't told any of us right away, and I was sure it was some kind of trick to stop us from bringing Catina back after all.

The thing was, as eager as I'd been to believe Persephone that Hades wasn't a real villain, it was so easy to look back to my previous beliefs and decide that Hades meant for this to happen. Why else would he not tell us right away Elyse died? Why not tell us the moment she lost another life? And how had she perished? Everyone said it had been an accident, but I was starting to wonder if Hades had been involved. All we heard was that he'd saved her, but I had doubts over his intentions.

Yes, it was unfair of me. But old habits died hard, and Hades didn't make it easy for anyone to think well of him.

We all congregated at Heracles's place. He was willing to host us while we prepared to go to the Underworld. But even though Hades wouldn't be with us, Heracles refused to accompany us.

I didn't blame him. He'd performed his twelve acts of valor, and he survived Hera's attacks. None of us expected him to get involved in a fight that had nothing to do with him.

"Don't get stuck in the Asphodel Meadows. There, you're not going to remember anything about the life you have on Earth. You'll forget everything you've ever fought for and not see a reason to leave." Heracles was trying to break down the Underworld to Elyse. We all knew what it was like down there—at least, we understood the concept. None of us gods had actually been there, aside from Heracles.

But Elyse had been there according to Heracles, except he hadn't taken her deep into the Underworld, not over the river. And the Greek myths were taught in school didn't exactly cover the layout of the Under-world. No human could really know what it was like since the souls that went to there never returned.

"What do I do?" Elyse asked. "Get across the river, and then...?"

"You have to get past that god-awful dog of Hades's, but I think you should be okay, as he only goes after the dead," Heracles continued. "And then you should be able to enter Hades's home. He lives on neutral ground. That's where X will be hiding—if he takes Catina anywhere else, she dies. And for that same reason, as long as you're close to one of the gods, Elyse, you should be okay until you reach that safe ground."

X had found a loophole in the Underworld. It was understandable; he lived there. We were the ones who hadn't taken the time to find out what it was like, to know if it was plausible he'd even be able to take a living human down to hell.

"We've got it covered," Ares stated, staring out the window.

He was dressed for war, wearing his armor, his leather, his sword. Next to me, Apollo also wore his leather, his body draped with weapons. We had to travel down there, retrieve Catina, and get back up here without any incident. I didn't want Elyse involved in any more fighting than absolutely necessary.

And knowing X, he planned on just that.

"Hey," Heracles called to Elyse, putting his hands on

her shoulders, forcing her to look up at him. "You're going to be just fine."

"How do you know?" Elyse wondered, and doubt threaded her voice.

"Because I know you. I've watched you and your family for years. I know who you are and what you're capable of. You need to believe in yourself now."

Elyse eyes narrowed, though the lines across her brow told me she worried a lot. Heracles had been there since the beginning, and she trusted him. He could convince her better than any of the rest of us could.

"Are we ready?" I asked when everyone was dressed and had their weapons strapped on. Ares was practicing his punching moves. Elyse had two swords crossed on her back and her scythe in her hand. She also wore a dark outfit, but it wasn't leather. Rather, the outfit offered her a bit of protection—it had supernatural material from Olympus woven by Athena, not too different than a bulletproof vest that would keep her safe from at least one blow of something serious before she'd have to deal with the aftermath.

Elyse had never felt the need to fight with armor before, but she was destabilized now. Her magic remained a little out of control, and she was aware of how vulnerable it made her. I wished we had more time for her to train, to become comfortable with her new magic.

But this was exactly what X had intended. To strip her of power, the ability she controlled. He'd taken the risk her new energy might be something she'd use against him and it had paid off.

But she wasn't going down there alone. We were all with her, and we were angry as fuck. Nothing was going to happen to her, not on our watch.

We'd suggested she take at least a little longer to recover after her death, but she had refused. And I understood—Catina's time was running out. X wouldn't keep her alive forever.

"Let's go," Apollo said, turning to Ares and me.

"I tried to find a way to join you, but Zeus has forbidden it." Heracles's gaze fell momentarily. "Good luck," he mumbled before we left his house.

I took Elyse's hand and the four of us vanished out of Chicago, reappearing in a cloudy mist, suspended in the sky.

The Underworld didn't have an entrance the way a lot of the Greek mythologies suggested. In the days of old, everyone had though there were entrances and exits to hell. But it was much simpler than that. All we had to do to get there was descend. I held Elyse's hand tighter while Ares took her other one, and when we descended, she came with us. Along with Apollo.

Immediately, we arrived on the banks of the River Styx. The black water rippled as if a breeze sailed over its surface. The river stretched outward as far as I could see, and directly across from us stood the side we needed to reach. Charon, the ferryman, sat on a chair looking out over the dark water. We were in a cabin made of stone, the gray slate on the walls smooth and slick with condensation.

"Well, I'm welcoming a lot of living company these days," Charon groused with sarcasm. "What do you guys want?"

"We need to get to the Underworld," I demanded, stepping forward.

"Sorry, that's not going to happen," the ferryman snorted, glancing at me. Then he frowned when he recognized me, and he straightened his posture as if he'd been caught misbehaving. "On the other hand," he cleared his throat—"I'm pretty sure Hades's brother is welcome. I guess, get in."

He pointed to his ferry, and I nodded, unsure Hades would be okay with me being in the Underworld—I wasn't exactly on his guest list. But anything to get past the river.

The five of us climbed onto the ferry and took a seat, facing the front. Charon followed and sat in the back. He started the engine.

"I thought you used an oar," Elyse said.

Charon chuckled. "Do you think we don't keep up with the times? Ferrying the souls across the river all the time is much easier when you have a motor."

Ares had mentioned the ferryman was arrogant,

and I saw what he was talking about. But Ares had a way of bringing out the worst out in people. He wasn't exactly the most tolerable guy, either. So, knowing him, he'd rubbed Charon the wrong way.

The motor was surprisingly quiet, but we glided across the river at a decent speed. While we moved, I looked at the water around us. It seemed dark and dangerous, and it was unclear what lay underneath. I was pretty sure if anyone who wasn't already dead fell in, they'd feel the consequences. Elyse was looking too, and she trembled.

"Here we are," the ferryman announced when we reached the other side of the river that divided the living world from the Underworld. "I brought you this far. Don't blame me if you don't get past the dog."

"Cerberus," Elyse said.

She knew her Greek mythology—all the Lowes had studied it to understand what they were up against, the monsters they had to defeat, and many of the legends. Heracles had captured the three-headed dog with Hades's approval, showed the mutt to King Eury as part of the quest, then returned the dog to the Underworld. Cerberus now guarded the gates of this realm so none of the souls escaped.

We climbed out of the boat, me first, guiding Elyse behind me. Ares leaped out next, while Apollo followed last. Charon flopped down in the boat and stared out into the river, waiting for our return.

We strode carefully across the stretch of black rock, our shadows flickering on walls pebbled with fiery torches. A haunting hum of voices sang in the distance, and my skin crawled. The songs of the dead were said to be hypnotize anyone who listened to them too long.

As we neared the gates of the Underworld, the humming faded, replaced with barking.

"Here we go," Apollo said, shaking himself, almost bouncing on his toes. Elyse pushed ahead, gripping her scythe. She never once wavered, and I couldn't have been prouder of her.

We closed in on enormous golden gates with an elaborate iron sculpture of Cerberus's head attached to the front, because of course Hades would decorate the place with images of his most treasured pet.

When we pushed open the gates, Cerberus emerged from a cloud of shadows and charged toward us.

Elyse gasped as the animal easily reached her waist.

The three heads were all looked at us, their lips curled away from sharp teeth. The serpents tail swung back and forth rhythmically, and his body was oily and dark, riddled with muscle.

Elyse jumped back, but the dog didn't attack. It halted a foot from us, growling, saliva drooling from his mouths.

"He's only here to stop the dead from leaving," Apollo informed us. "He should let us pass."

Elyse eyed the animal and gave him a wide berth.

"I'd rather not take that chance. And didn't you hear Charon's threat?"

"Hell, man, I'm ready to fight it if we need to," Ares declared, staring at the snarling dog. The mutt leaped toward Ares, three sets of mouths snapping at the air, inches from his pants, and he flinched. Apollo chuckled.

I tucked Elyse against my side, holding her around the waist. "Ares, you'll get your chance, but not against Hades's pet."

We made our way around the dog. I kept myself between Elyse and Cerberus just in case. He dog growled and barked, snapping at the air between us, but he hadn't sensed death on any of us, as he didn't attack. Getting in easy seemed easy enough, but perhaps getting out wouldn't be so simple.

We passed Cerberus and reached the neutral ground Heracles had spoken of. Hades had built himself a castle on this rock, a palace of darkness. When I looked up at it, I stiffened, studying a magnificent mansion—even if it was dreary. Everything was black. Part of the rock it had been built with glowed red, as if fashioned from embers. The very embers of hell.

This was where Hades had lived since he'd been banished to the Underworld to rule. It was where Persephone had been forced to live for half the year after Hades tricked her into staying with him.

Since we'd deceived Hades into the Underworld in

the first place, I felt terrible about what we'd done. At the time, it seemed like a funny joke—a prank that would trump all other pranks. I hadn't thought it would mean Hades's banishment from Mount Olympus for the rest of eternity purely because he didn't reign there.

As the centuries had continued on, the gravity of my mistake started to weight on my heart and mind. Or at least, so I'd thought.

Now, as we moved toward Hades's palace, I grew overwhelmed by sorrow and guilt. Tightness coiled around my chest and limbs, and my heart ached. A wave of self-loathing filled me, leaving me unable to concentrate on anything else. This horrible place, filled with darkness and despair and the stench of decay, was what I'd doomed my brother to for all eternity.

It made sense why he remained so upset with us, why he couldn't drop his grudge. I would've done so much worse had I been in his shoes.

What had we done? Could some of the shit going on with X also be partially Zeus's and my fault too? Forcing our brother down here until he snapped?

Apollo and Ares stared at the place with wide eyes, convincing me they shared my sentiments.

"I think the Fates are here to greet us," Elyse cautioned when three women appeared at the grand double doors.

"Agreed," I said, recognizing the three witches, and

clenching my jaw. Nothing good ever came from being told riddles about the future.

As we approached, it became clear that only one of them could see. The other two were completely blind, wearing blindfolds over their eyes. The Fates shared one eye, taking turns to look at the past, the present, and the future.

Elyse shivered against me, and I noted that Apollo and Ares let me step forward first.

"We've been expecting you," said the first Fate, the one with the eye.

Of course. They'd known we were coming.

"And we have a message for you," continued another with a croaky voice.

"Only when you accept your flaws are you strong enough to overcome them," the third instructed.

Ares groaned. "We're not here for some fortune cookie bullshit. We're here for the human girl."

"Oh, we know why you're here." They spoke in unison, which was downright creepy.

"None of us know if you'll ever escape," one of the blind Fates said.

Elyse glanced at me, fear clear on her face, and I felt it in my gut. Apollo marched on her other side, taking her hand in his, standing guard. Letting fear into my thoughts would be the quickest way to fail.

"Come on," I ordered. "We'll get out of here as soon as we find what we've come for."

"We just hope that what you came for is what you find," one of them said.

They always talked in riddles, and everything they said carried a deeper meaning, I just had to work out what they meant. But if this was the company Hades had to keep and the more I saw of the Underworld, the worse I felt about what I'd done to him.

CHAPTER 22

Ares

The Underworld wasn't my favorite place to be. Goosebumps slithered down my arms, and I hated that we had to go farther than that ferryman who kept running his mouth. But we were all here for Elyse, to save Catina, and there was no turning back now.

As if that Hound of Hades hadn't been eerie enough, now we'd run into the three Fates. Three old witches with one eye shared among them? Who'd come up with that shit? Of course, I'd heard of the Fates many times, but I was one of the few gods who hadn't actually run into them personally. Until now.

I'd made a point of staying away from them. They couldn't cast me out if I wasn't there. It was the motto

I'd lived by for a very long time. And it had worked so far.

But I'd changed that rule—for Elyse. In fact, it was only because of her that I'd started seeing myself as part of the team. And even though it wasn't nearly as bad as I thought it'd be, there were definitely a few things I could've done without.

The trip to the Underworld was definitely at the top of the list at this point. I was creeped out.

"Do we have to go in there?" I asked when we'd passed the Fates and stood in front of the large doors that led into the palace. The whole building was black with red lights that pulsed like a heartbeat. It was ironic, considering everyone who came here—aside from Hades, Persephone, X, and the Fates—were dead.

Maybe it was supposed to be a joke. The palace was the only heartbeat around.

"I bet she's at the top of the tallest tower," Apollo said.

Like this was some kind of fairy tale. But he was probably right. X had a dark sense of humor and turning this into something that humans were familiar with would be right up his alley.

"So, I guess that's a *yes* to going inside," I remarked when no one had answered my question.

Maybe they'd thought it had been rhetorical. And maybe it had been. We'd come here for Catina, and we weren't leaving without her.

Dead or alive.

I shivered when I thought that. Alive. We'd definitely get her back alive.

As soon as we stepped into the palace, a chill ran down my spine. The place was a representation of death. Everything was carved from black stone. Mirrors hung everywhere, and it gave a house of horrors effect. Here and there, the pulsing red parts of the stones showed. How fucking depressing.

As we walked through the rooms, we encountered occasional cutesy heart shaped decorations, candles everywhere, and some random pieces of tasteful furniture. But none of it made up for the horrible feeling of doom that hung in the air.

How had Hades held out down here? If I had to spend an eternity in a place like this, I was pretty sure I'd get creative about finding a way to end the life of an immortal. Namely me.

We traveled down every hall and checked every room we passed, discovering more tasteful furniture. But no X.

Down here, darkness reigned, and we couldn't tell X apart from any of the other shadows. When we were about halfway through the palace, going from room to room, each lavishly decorated and ready for guests, I looked out one of the windows.

In front of me lay the Asphodel Meadows. To my left were the Fields of Mourning where those with broken hearts ended up, and to my right, Tartarus, reserved for those who'd sinned in their lives, who didn't deserve pardon.

And on the horizon—if the Underworld had a horizon—were the Fields of Elysium. It was where the heroes were allowed to reside, and where Elyse's entire family awaited her. It was technically part of the Underworld, but not really. I read a lot of books in my spare time.

Elyse came to stand next to me and glanced out across the areas beneath us, beyond to the Fields. I knew she was thinking about her family, about where she was going when she died one more time. If X didn't get her first.

I took her hand and kissed her knuckles. "Not today," I said.

She only nodded, but her breath hitched. I hoped she believed that we'd succeed as much as I did. But her fear danced over my flesh like a bitter cold. She was worried. Silence and tension permeated the air between us, and there were only grim faces among the group. My stomach tightened.

"Let's keep moving." Poseidon broke the quiet.

I turned, and Elyse followed.

It took us a while to work our way through the palace, moving up and up. Always silent. Never finding Catina. The farther we traveled, the fewer rooms there were to inspect until we found the spiral staircase that led up to what could only be the tallest tower.

How ironic. And Apollo had called it.

When we arrived, the door was locked. It wasn't hard to break it down, though. I stepped up for the job and kicked my heel into the wooden door, the loud thud reverberating around us as the wood splintered and the door swung open inward.

And inside, like a princess who'd been closed up in the tower, Catina lay on a bed. She sat up, her watery eyes enlarged. Her skin looked clammy and glistened with a cold sweat. Her hair hung limp, and fear edged her face. But Elyse stepped around me, and Catina's face changed to relief. Her mouth slackened.

"Oh my God, I'm not even going to ask how you found me!" she cried, wrapping her arms around Elyse. The two women embraced, and the rest of us waited for them to get their emotions out of the way.

"I'm so sorry. We came as soon as we tracked you down." Elyse's voice crackled with emotions.

"What the hell took me?" Catina's chin trembled.

"A fuckhead. Have you not seen him since you were taken?" Elyse asked.

Catina looked around as if expecting a monster to jump out of the shadows. "I was locked in here with food and water and nothing else to go by. Where are we? This place is like hell on Earth."

"Or hell in hell," Elyse said. "This is the Underworld."

Catina's head flinched back slightly. "What do you mean?"

"I'll explain later." Elyse rushed her words and kept

glancing at the boarded-up windows. "We have to get you out of here. Now."

"Who are they?" Catina asked when she walked with Elyse toward us. She looked up with uncertainty, with caution.

Elyse sighed. "This is Poseidon, Ares, and Apollo. The guys I'm dating."

Catina looked from us to Elyse and shook her head. "I don't get it."

Of course she wouldn't. Not only did it sound like a silly joke, but everything about this was difficult to believe. From the moment Catina had been taken, nothing would have made sense to her anymore. How could it have?

"We have to go," I told Elyse, holding out my hand. She cleared her throat and took my hand, letting me guide her out of the tower. Catina followed, flanked on both sides by Poseidon and Apollo. The five of us had to get out of here alive.

We made our way all the way to the bottom floor of the palace without incident. I stopped and turned to Apollo and Poseidon.

"Something's wrong," I whispered. "This was too easy. X hasn't even tried to stop us."

"He will," Elyse muttered.

"You're absolutely right," a voice said behind us and we all spun around. Catina let out a scream riddled with terror, faced with the person who'd taken her captive. She sank to the ground, crippled by her own fear.

Apollo, Poseidon, and I stepped forward, ready to attack. Elyse stayed right next to us, willing to fight, even though she struggled with her power. But she wouldn't let anything happen to Catina, not now we'd found her.

X laughed, his hissing voice grated on my nerves, and he looked at the four of us.

"What a band of misfits," he sneered. "It's cute you thought you could save her. But I'm glad you tried."

With that, he attacked. But it wasn't the physical contact I'd expected. Instead, a cloud of darkness rose around us until it was almost impossible to see each other, to see him.

"Elyse!" I cried out.

"I'm right here," she said, grabbing on to me.

She carried her scythe in a sheath on her back, and she was ready to use it. Maybe she would. But right now, it was about our power against X's.

I focused on my magic, the ability buzzing over my nape, and I let it flare up. I sensed Apollo and Poseidon do the same, the electricity around us heightening. When Elyse tried, her power vacillated, coming and going, and X chuckled. He sensed it, too.

"Really, you shouldn't have bothered bringing her along. She just weighs you down. Now you have two humans to look after, and it'll only cripple you."

Elyse attacked first. She let out a battle cry and

swung her scythe through the air with practiced precision. I mirrored her and jumped in on her heels. Her power might not have been as controlled as before, but she was still a seasoned fighter, and she'd trained for most of her life. X hadn't expected us to attack so vehemently, and we managed to catch him off guard, sending him recoiling backward. Excellent.

The fight was immediately brutal. As soon as X recovered from his surprise, he retaliated, and Elyse was in over her head. X was stronger and faster than her, and she needed help.

Apollo charged in, but Poseidon hung back, taking care of Catina. He had the power to call any of his weapons, so he was best suited to protect her, and I was glad he'd taken the initiative. On the battlefield, we could only rely on what we did naturally. Hesitating would be our downfall.

The fight grew intense, and Elyse wielded her weapon. X ducked and kicked her in the gut, then unleashed another round of magic, slamming into her. She grunted and withdrew a few steps, but she never fell. She wasn't handling her new magic very well. I moved out, staying at her side, mimicking her movements. I'd trained with her a couple of times and was familiar with her routines, the rhythm she found, the way she jumped from one side to the other before doubling back. We were a team, fighting X together. Apollo attacked from the side, his bright energy colliding into X, but we weren't bringing him down.

When Poseidon realized we weren't winning, he made sure that Catina was out of the way before he jumped in and fought alongside us, too. All three of us and Elyse stood together, fighting X as one.

The unity should have had an effect, just like the powerful strength we generated when the three of us touched. Our ability should have grown, become stronger than X, overpowered him. But somehow, we still failed. We stood together, and we fought hard, but it wasn't having much of an impact.

This was what I did best. I was the God of War—I loved to battle. When in combat, no matter the cause, I was happiest. Partly because I knew I was good at it, and partly because I usually won.

But this time, we'd lose. The knowledge hit me square in the chest, and spilled cold sensation right through me.

X laughed, his fiery eyes locked on mine. "It doesn't matter where you are, God of War, your mind will always be your worst enemy. The moment you believe you've lost, you already have."

No, he was wrong. This wasn't the end. It couldn't be. Because if it were the end, Elyse and Catina would die. The three gods would go back empty-handed, and that would only kill us on the inside.

"Of course," he added with a chuckle. "Even if you think you'll win, you won't. You're on my turf now, and what I say goes. This is the Underworld. This is where Death rules."

CHAPTER 23

Hades

I paced my bedroom, unable to settle down. The others were in the Underworld. I felt them, almost as if they were a footprint on my soul. They were there to rescue the human girl. And Elyse had joined them.

From the moment they arrived, and the ferryman allowed them to pass, assuming my brother should be allowed, I'd sensed them.

But why hadn't I sensed X or the human he'd taken into my house? If I knew it was where he'd hidden her, I would've told Elyse.

Contrary to what everyone seemed to believe, I didn't want anyone to get hurt. I cared about every-thing that went wrong. Granted, I hadn't been acting that way. I pretended I didn't give a shit. It was the easiest way to get everyone to leave me alone.

If I didn't care, I remained safe. The fact I wasn't able to stop caring was beside the point.

I'd experienced Elyse's happiness when she'd found her friend, beaming in my chest like a ray of sunshine on my face. I'd felt the determination of the three gods to get out of there as soon as possible.

And I felt the tightening of my gut when X cornered them and started a fight they couldn't win.

X wouldn't be able to do anything to the three gods. We were all immortal, and we couldn't hurt each other physically, just emotionally. Denting our egos. Of course, that hurt like a bitch, too. But it didn't kill us.

Sometimes, I wished it did.

But X could kill Elyse's friend. He'd obliterate her and force her soul to remain in the Underworld, no matter what the others did.

And he'd kill Elyse. And if he murdered her this time, she'd be dead for good. She wouldn't come back again. Elyse had died as many times as she was able to recover from. When my brother bestowed his power on the Lowe bloodline, he'd only given them a finite number of lives before they'd die their final death. They weren't immortal.

Technically, they weren't even demigods.

Elyse could die. And that was what X intended. I heard his call for her death, his fury at her power as distinctly as if it were my own. He was burning with rage to finish her. And my stomach rolled as invisible fingers snaked down my spine at the thought of what X planned for her.

I didn't want Elyse dead, losing her mortal life. She'd trained so hard, took pride in what she did. I wanted her radiating with joy, laughing, and wearing her gorgeous smile.

But the group was losing against X, and if I wanted it to stop, I would have to go down there and get involved. If I decided to stand against X, who essentially just a version of myself, it would mean openly accepting how I felt about Elyse. Acknowledging she'd taken a piece of my heart, that I craved more than anything to admit my feelings and no longer conceal them. No more hiding or running away.

Nausea surged through me. I couldn't do that. All this time, I pushed away how I felt about her because I couldn't afford to get hurt again. And I'd dealt with too much of that over the past millennia. I'd opened myself up to heartbreak and grief, and I'd fucking had enough.

I couldn't do it anymore.

I stalked to the wet bar adjacent to my living room and poured myself three fingers of whiskey. The humans turned to this stuff all the time when they were in emotional turmoil. I could see the appeal. Somehow, the mortals believed it would change the course of fate if they drank enough. I wasn't that stupid. But I'd drink myself into a state of oblivion, and I wouldn't know what happened while I was out.

I wouldn't feel when Elyse died.

Hollowness swallowed me, and my pulse slowed. I rested my head on one hand and breathed deeply.

"You're an idiot," Persephone said, appearing next to me. I jumped and nearly dropped my glass.

"Fuck. Don't sneak up on me like that, woman. You'll give me a heart attack."

"Maybe a heart attack is exactly what you need to jumpstart that thing. Because it must have stopped beating at some point for you to be okay with what's going on."

She lifted her perfectly shaped eyebrows at me and folded her arms over her chest.

Of course she sensed the shit tornado coming. The Underworld was her home as much as mine, and she felt the intruders as well.

"She's going to die, Hades. Don't you care?" she asked when I didn't respond.

I threw back the contents of my glass and let the amber goodness burn down my throat. "I'm not going." I poured more whiskey, not stopped bothering to count how many fingers and filled it to the top. If I planned to get drunk, why do it half a glass at a time?

"You love her," Persephone insisted.

Her words stabbed me in the chest.

"Dammit, Persephone, what do you want from me?"

"I want you to man up and accept what's going on here. Are you just going to hide in your little corner until it's too late? This is not the man I know you are."

I downed the contents of my glass, my throat on fire. "And what do you know about the man I am? How can you say you know anything about me when the person you knew was only the result of a curse?"

Persephone sighed and glared at me. "You can't hold on to that forever. It was millennia ago. Yes, Hera pulled a fast one on you. And you got caught up in something you didn't want. But guess what? So did I. And you don't see me moping around and wishing ill on everyone around me, do you?"

She was right. I'd tricked her into staying in the Underworld for half the year, the same place I held a grudge against my brothers for tricking me into. Essentially, I'd done the same to her. But she wasn't miserable and bitter like me.

"Maybe you're just a better person than I am." I meant it, since I was hardly the kind of man worth loving. And Persephone had proven that by not returning my love, no matter how hard she tried.

"You have to accept how you feel about Elyse," Persephone pressed. "If you don't, you're going to lose her, and that's going to hurt a hell of a lot more than anything else that's happened to you."

I put the glass down on the bar and dragged myself to the couch in the living room, before sitting down and dropping my head into my hands. My world spun, my heart lay shattered, and I was torn in two.

"They're not doing well down there," I muttered. I didn't really care if Persephone heard me, if she was listening or not.

"So? Go help them then." She sat next to me.

I shook my head in my hands. "I can't. I'm not going down there. She doesn't want me."

"Bullshit, Hades," Persephone snapped, and I looked at her, shocked at the kind of language coming from her beautiful mouth. Through it all, Persephone had always remained sophisticated, ladylike. I'd morphed into the dirtiest, foulest person because of my circumstances, but Persephone had held her head up high.

"You know she needs you," she continued. "You know they're losing down there, and if X gets the upper hand—which will be soon—Elyse is going to be dead. And you'll lose her forever."

"I'm not just talking about this fight," I began. "I mean, as someone in her life. As a lover. Elyse doesn't need me. Look at me. Who I've become. She doesn't deserve this." I pictured her smile and how I'd told myself I had to help her survive...then move on with my life. Except, I wasn't sure I could do that.

Persephone's eyes were soft, filled with an inner glow. "That I actually agree with. You're a mess, and you'll have to prove yourself to her. I wouldn't push you to go after her if I didn't believe you merit love. The thing is, she loves you, too. Everyone can see it.

And you need to start accepting this is how it is. You may be able to turn yourself down, but it's a crime to turn her away. Especially if she can see who you are through this horrible facade you put on for everyone."

"But she has so many other gods to keep her busy," I argued. "Even Poseidon, my own brother. I wouldn't be surprised if she got in there with Heracles, too. But you know how he is, in love with only one."

"Oh, for Zeus's sake, Hades!" Persephone cried out. "Every time I think you can't become more pathetic...I know I hurt you. I tried to make us work, I really did. I believed you deserved love when you'd been cursed, and I tried to give it to you. It's on me that I failed. But don't let that stop you from loving again. And stop lying to yourself. You'll do Elyse good if you just go and help her. Be a hero for once."

I met her gaze. Her eyes were dark and deep and serious. She sat on my couch, telling me how I should be, telling me to man up and do what I needed to do. And she was right. I hated admitting it about my ex, but Persephone knew exactly what she was talking about.

I opened my mouth to say something in return, but she disappeared. She'd said her piece and had no reason to stick around.

But she was right.

I had to stop this fight before it was too late. The darkness grew, the gods were losing, and Elyse was weakening. She wasn't in control of her power and X was suffocating her with his energy, which had already taken root inside her after her three deaths. The bite mark he'd left on her weeks ago, which had spread and left black marks on her flesh, connected with his energy; it gave him a foundation to hook into her. The bastard knew what he was doing.

I'd fucked around too long, too scared to make a decision, but it felt crystal clear in my head now. My heart pounded for Elyse, to bring her the joy she deserved. And for me to man up already.

The moment I decided to help her, I was there, in my palace in the Underworld. A shiver curled over my nape as it always did when I returned home. But I had no time to focus on how much I loathed the place. I faced X. The others stood behind me, Elyse driven to her knees.

"Oh, look who came to join the party," X gibed with a smug smile, his fangs exposed.

"Leave them alone," I said to him. "You have no right to do this."

I attacked X before he had a chance to answer. And immediately, the darkness shattered around us, as if it had been fragile all along. I knew what was happening —X lost the moment I determined to accept how I felt about Elyse. I wasn't ready to lose her. I'd deal with the repercussions of that decision later. Right now, Elyse needed saving.

The moment the others sensed X's power slipping, they ran to my side.

"I'm glad you could join us," Poseidon commented next to me. He had an expression on his face I didn't quite understand. "Thank you for coming, brother."

I couldn't remember the last time Poseidon had called me "brother." It was as if he really cared. I wasn't sure what had changed his mind about me. And with it came a light-hearted feeling that maybe all wasn't lost between us.

"How are we going to end this?" Apollo asked, clapping palms with me after Ares did.

"Together." I looked over my shoulder. "Elyse, get out of here. We'll finish up."

Elyse stared at me, a look of shock on her face. She hadn't expected to see me here. But there was only one way I could change her mind about me, and that was to show her.

"I'm staying to fight." She squared her shoulders, lifting her chin defiantly.

"You've done all you can. We need to work out how to stuff X back into the box where he belongs. It's up to us now. And I owe my fair share of fixing this shit for a change."

She stared at me for a long pause, almost convincing me she'd fight me on this. Except, I spoke the truth. The battle would simply be about gods's energy against energy, otherwise I'd welcome Elyse to fight alongside me. She could fight as well as any of us.

Finally, she nodded and helped her friend off the ground. "Come on. We're going home," she said. She glanced at me one more time before I wrapped her in my power to send them back to Earth. A moment later, Catina and Elyse disappeared.

"Right." I nodded when the four of us were alone. "Let's wrap this up."

CHAPTER 24

Elyse

A week had passed since we'd rescued Catina. In some ways, it felt like it had only been yesterday. In others, it felt like a lifetime ago. The gods had taken on X for Hades to regain control over him, something I couldn't do with them because I wasn't a god. Whatever! But in the end, they failed, and X escaped their clutches. The monster had eaten so many souls, leaving him close to unstoppable.

So, the five us would need to work as a solid team to find a way to overcome him. And while it sucked he got away, part of me couldn't stop thinking about Hades's decision to finally join our fight, to stop hiding and take responsibility. My heart beamed that he was on our side for a change. So even though we hadn't won yet, we'd gained Hades in a way. And he was the key to ending X's killing spree. That gave me hope to believe we could win, and a reminder not let myself drown in sorrow, and to keep fighting, to have faith in a bright future and not to forget to do the simplest things like smile. Otherwise, X had indeed won.

Since we'd all returned to Earth, I'd started training again. I learned how to control myself more than ever. After all, I needed to keep myself safe—I couldn't die again. Knowing I could recover after death had been a kind of buffer I didn't realize I'd relied on. I'd been fearless, charging headlong into battle, because I figured I wouldn't die permanently.

But that was over. This time, if I died, it'd be the end. So I had to make sure that didn't happen.

"Right, let's begin/" Heracles entered into the training center. I'd already warmed up.

"Great of you to join us," I joked.

Heracles was in town now and then. He kept his word, saying he was going to do hero work, and he helped the humans out where he could through his secret vigilante ways. I mean he was a god, and no human stood a chance against him. But if it brought him joy to carry out heroic work, all the power to him.

And Heracles was enjoying himself keeping the humans safe. It was what he'd done for a long time, ages ago. How he had made a living, and how he'd ended up meeting Megara, the love of his life. It brought me joy he'd found a path for himself. All this time, I'd assumed he'd been sneaking out to date, except he'd been dealing with his own demons his way. And I respected that a lot.

"What weapons have you ordered?" he asked.

"Nothing new. I figured I went through so many great weapons before, it would be a good idea to make sure I can wield all of them. It doesn't help to be a jack of all trades, but master of none."

Heracles chuckled. "You humans and your silly sayings."

I picked lint from my top. "Ready to get started? Or are you scared?"

He laughed out loud, throwing his head back. I loved seeing him like this. In the beginning, he never smiled and laughed as much as he did now. He truly was happy, and I wanted that for him.

"Scared?" he repeated. "Me? Did you forget who I am?"

"Nope." I dropped into a battle stance. "But you seem to have forgotten who I am. I'm Elyse Lowe, protector of the humans, appointed by Zeus. And this isn't going to be an easy fight."

My words had barely left my mouth when I attacked, spinning around and kicking Heracles in the chest when he'd expected a punch.

"Oh, look at you, veering from your normal routine. I like it."

"Me, too," I said. "Predictable will get me killed. And I'm trying to avoid that now."

"It took a long time for you to get there," he added

between punches. "But I'm glad you're starting to see it that way."

"I have to," I responded before spinning around and aiming for his knee. "I still have a job to do here on Earth. I can't die yet."

Heracles and I did some hand-to-hand combat, sparring and bantering back and forth before we got serious. I took my weapons from my duffel bag, and laid them out before us. I decided to begin on one end and work my way through. It would take a day, but I didn't mind training for hours on end.

X was still out there.

The four gods hadn't provided in-depth details of the battle, except to say it was a tug-a-war of their godly power, and X was stronger than any of them could have guessed. Ares did mention that if I was there, X would have drawn my energy and probably killed me. I preferred to imagine that they had beaten him to a pulp, showing him what it was like to go up against four gods who were serious about who they were protecting.

Unfortunately, Hades hadn't been able to reel X in, despite how he'd managed to shatter the darkness. Whatever Hades still had to work through, X was free and using his freedom to dominate the world. He'd laid low for a while, but it was only a matter of time before he struck again. So I asked the gods to keep a vigilant eye over Catina as well as staying close to me.

Until X resurfaced, I'd train, mastering my power,

getting used to the magic I could wield and practicing with every weapon I owned. When the day came that X showed his face again, I'd be ready. And I hoped to have four gods at my back.

"So," Heracles said when we took a water break. "Have you spoken to Hades lately?"

Heracles knew how I felt about Hades—he'd been the first person I'd talked to about developing feelings for the god of the Underworld and Apollo, way back when they first arrived on Earth. Damn, that felt like a lifetime ago. Three, actually. I smirked at my own lame joke.

I swallowed the water. "No, he disappeared. I went to his place a couple of times, but he hasn't been around. I'm starting to think maybe he stayed in the Underworld—perhaps finding a way to finally eradicate X. I want to give him space until he's ready to come back."

When I said that, a pang of sorrow shot into my chest. More than anything, I wished for Hades to return to Earth. I wanted to see more of him, to talk him.

I couldn't help but feel like him staying away was partly my fault. But there wasn't much I could do about it. If Hades intended to be scarce, I'd have to wait for him to come back.

If he ever did.

"Just give him time," Heracles said. "The downside of being alive for eternity is not really having a concept of time. Give him what he needs, and I think he'll return."

My throat grew scratchy. I hoped he would. I didn't say so out loud. Instead, I picked up my scythe. "Have you seen me work with this?" I asked. "I'm pretty decent with it."

Heracles chuckled. "I haven't, but I bet you're going to show me."

And I did.

Heracles and I trained for six hours straight before he finally told me he had to go.

"I have to go see my dad," he explained.

"You're meeting with Zeus a lot lately," I pointed out.

His lips pressed together in a light grimace, and that worried me. "We have a lot to discuss. Maybe one day, I'll tell you what it's about. But I can share this—he's proud of who you've become."

It would have been great if Zeus came and told me himself. In the beginning, when I'd been unsure about who I was, he visited me. But now he remained on Mount Olympus, and I had to trudge through my self-doubt alone.

Although I wasn't truly my own. I had Apollo, Ares, and Poseidon—and from Heracles, who was, and always would be a great hero.

"Will I see you tomorrow for another workout?" I asked.

He shook his head. "I have to go out of town. But I'll

send Ares. I hear you two get along just fine." He winked at me.

I smiled and my cheeks heated, which was so unlike me. But there was no denying my reaction or his words. It was true, Ares and I made a great team. Who else did a fighter need but the God of War to practice with? Plus, we always got down to some different kind of exercise when we were finished. And I became hot just thinking about our time together.

"Well, I'll see you around." But I hesitated and instead of walking away, I approached Heracles and hugged him. I looped my arms around his solid torso, resting my cheek against his chest.

He stiffened at first, then embraced me in return and chuckled. "What's this all about?"

"Life's short. I don't want to regret anything."

He rubbed my back, and I pulled away. "See you later." And I left the center while he remained behind, doing God-knew-what.

I climbed in my car and drove to Catina's place. Since she'd returned, she'd taken a few days off work, and Tina allowed it. I told Catina I'd reported her as a missing person, and she was dealing with her boss and the local journalists insisting on hearing her story. Of course, she turned them all down and stuck with the story of not remembering who abducted her and that he must have released her one day because she woke up in the woods.

With Apollo's approval, I gifted her with his necklace. The essence of the moon shone light in the darkest of times and repelled X in a way. So maybe it would offer Catina a few extra moments for escape or to call me if the monster returned.

When I knocked on her door, I called out, "It's me."

Since X had taken Catina, even though he had simply appeared in the room, she was nervous about everyone who knocked on her door. It was understandable; being kidnapped was traumatic in and of itself. Being abducted by some kind of immortal God, demon, or whatever made it much worse.

Catina opened the door and hugged me, her body slightly shaky. "I'm so glad you're here. I was starting to get lonely. I don't like being alone these days."

"I had to finish working out with Heracles." It felt amazing to use his real name, rather than keep secrets from my friend.

Since Catina realized I wasn't exactly human, I'd told her everything. That my mentor wasn't just any old personal coach, but Heracles, son of Zeus himself. That the four men I'd been involved with were gods.

"Did Apollo pop over earlier as I promised?" I asked, wanting her to know someone was always looking out for her, and she didn't have to live in fear.

She sighed loudly, fingering Apollo's pendant around her neck. "He's eaten nearly half the food in the fridge. How much does he eat?"

I laughed.

"I still can't believe what's happening," Catina said

after we sat down in the living room with coffee. "You're training with Heracles. You say it like it's nothing. But it's still impossible to wrap my mind around. And your whole family? I've known you since high school and somehow you've hidden yourself from me completely."

I smiled. "I couldn't exactly go running around telling everyone I was a hero. Kids get bullied at school for saying stuff like that."

She laughed. "Well, I'll forgive you for not sharing that kind of news with your best friend. How are the rest of your guys? Or should I say *gods*? Extremely sexy gods! I don't know how you control yourself around them. Just having Apollo lounge on my sofa had me in awe. Not that I was looking at him in that way, he's yours, but I mean…hell, he's hot."

I chuckled. "He is. And the rest of them are fine."

"Damn fine," Catina interjected, her eyebrows arching.

"You get used to it," I said, laughing.

"I don't know how. Those guys are hotter than anyone I've seen before. I understand now why you can't just choose one. No wonder you want to be with all of them."

I was still laughing. The fact they were gods wasn't what it was about, although it sure didn't hurt. And sleeping with them was amazing. But it was about how I felt around them, how they responded to me, how our powers linked up and became something bigger than when we were alone. I had a special connection with them all and I didn't want to sacrifice any one of them. They meant the world to me, and the more time I spent with them, the more I intended to do whatever I needed to keep them forever.

When all three of the gods were okay with me dating all of them, why did I have to change anything? They weren't all about exclusivity, and it worked for me. In some ways, I was so much more like them than I was like the humans.

"I'm not here to talk about me," I demurred, changing the topic. "I'm here to find out how you're doing."

Catina shivered and looked into her cup. "I guess I'm okay. I get nightmares that are full of darkness, and I can't help but see those fiery eyes. Whenever I see them, I try to turn away, but I always feel like I just can't help but fall into them."

I placed a hand on her arm, letting her know I was there for her. X had eyes that could control anyone's mind, and it was one of the ways he used to consume humans. Catina was lucky he hadn't destroyed her.

"Have you been staying at the apartment completely alone?" I inquired. She hadn't been back to work, and each time I spoke with her, she was home.

"Well, not completely alone." She glanced up at me. "Oliver's been keeping me company. He's coming over soon."

"What?" I asked in surprise. "Oliver?"

She shrugged again, blushing. "It turns out he's a really nice guy. We're getting along quite well." She hesitated, her lips pinching, and she studied me with a mischievous gaze. "We're kind of dating."

I shook my head, surprised but not shocked. "Are you being serious? It happened so quickly."

"Yeah. But you know how it is. When there's something that works, you just can't fight it."

I giggled. Had Catina just compared her relationship with Oliver to my relationship with the gods? But I understood what she was saying, and I was gushing with joy for her. I couldn't believe she was with Oliver, but she deserved a happy ending. The human one. As did he.

Catina and I would always be friends, even though she knew who I was now. She was still my connection to the human world, and despite being privy to the fact I carried some kind of godly power and dated three gods, we were still going to have girls' night and gossip.

The balance between my divine life and my human life was important. The gods gave me enough of one, and Catina somehow managed to stabilize it out with the other. The shit with X was far from over, but it was great to know I had one foot firmly in each world.

And now I knew who I was, I could figure out what I wanted from life. Plus, I was ready for whatever X had in mind for me.

Bring it on.

By the time I arrived home, Ares stood outside my

apartment, wearing the most mischievous grin, his blue eyes sparkling beneath the sun. Dressed in jeans that hung low on his hips, black boots, and a matching tee, he stretched a hand out toward me. His fingers curled around my wrist.

"Perfect timing." He drew me closer, and I tucked the car keys into my back pocket before falling against him.

"What do you have in mind?" I wrapped myself around him, loving how his body burned with heat. Damn, he smelled so musky and delicious. I lifted my gaze to find his grin widening, and a tingle fluttered in my gut. He was so gorgeous—from the glimmer of his eyes to the husky sound of his voice. My heart beat quicker as I pictured him stripping me and having his way with me once we got inside the apartment.

He ran a hand through my hair and cupped the back of my head before leaning down and kissing me. It was full, open-mouthed, and so hot, I quivered under him. His lips were fire, searing me in an instant. I let myself fall, adoring everything about him.

The world around us tilted, and I held on tight, because moments later, a cool breeze washed through my hair and I broke free from his hold.

We now stood in a parking area behind several blocks of apartments.

Farther to our right I spotted a white trailer with half a dozen people, mostly uniformed cops, waiting to be served by the man sticking out the side window taking orders on a notepad. The breeze swished past again, bringing with it the most delicious aroma of slow cooked beef roast and baked bread. My stomach rumbled for food.

"Where are we?" I loved when the gods whisked me away to different destinations and surprised me, because who the hell didn't love such devotion. My men were growing on me with each passing day, and I wanted them more than anything. Sure, at the back of my mind, I reminded myself they were freaking gods who lived forever, unlike me, but I refused to think about those implications. Not when for the first time I felt as if I finally belonged somewhere.

"California. They make the best tacos here. You've got to taste the fish ones."

I looked across at Ares, a hand flying to my chest as giddiness swarmed through me. "I love tacos."

He winked and looped an arm around my waist then hauled me against him. He walked us to an empty wooden table with upside down plastic milk crates for seats. "Take a load off. I won't be long." He stole a kiss lasting longer than a few seconds and swept me off my feet, literally, sucking on my lower lip. "You taste like candy," he breathed before lowering me to the ground and walked away to grab us food.

I flopped down on a crate, tingling all over, checking out Ares's ass in his jeans. Gnawing on my cheek, I had to pinch myself to believe I had such men in my life.

Police occupied the few tables around us, most of them chatting loudly, laughing. We must be near a police station.

Someone gave a wolf whistle behind me, and I turned around, along with half the officers.

Poseidon and Apollo strolled toward me, smirking, almost glowing beneath the sun that suddenly shone brighter in the clearest sky.

My heart skipped a beat to see them strutting closer, clear they'd planned this rendezvous with Ares, and that had me bubbling with excitement. After all the shit we'd gone through, I loved getting together with them over a meal.

While some of the cops returned to their food, a couple of the females at the table next to us eyed the newcomers, devouring them with their gazes. And who could blame them…? Hell, they were staring at gods.

But they were all mine, and my toes bounced under the table.

"Hey gorgeous," Apollo said, taking a seat next to me, planting a kiss on my lips, his hand on my back.

Poseidon sat on the other side of me, his fingers crawling over my thigh, and he leaned in, stealing a longer kiss. "Missed you."

I snuck a glance over the next table to where the ladies still gawked, and I wondered if their expressions were surprise along with jealousy that I'd snagged these incredible men all for myself.

"Of course, you all arrive as soon as the food gets

271

here," Ares declared, drawing my attention to him. He set a large tray filled with delicious tacos in the middle of the table—clearly he'd ordered far more than the two of us could eat.

Apollo chuckled and already reached for the food, as did Poseidon.

"Thanks guys." I grabbed a taco before they all vanished. "I needed this."

"I suggested we all meet in Italy for the best gelato, but I was outvoted." Apollo took a big bite of his taco.

"Or Shanghai for delicious soup dumplings." Poseidon glanced over at me and wriggled his eyebrows in such a devilish way, I leaned against him, loving how his warmth skipped over to me.

"Well, I organized this, so I got to pick," Ares said. "Next time, feel free." He gestured to the guys by waving his taco in their direction before taking a huge mouthful.

"Why here?" I asked.

He wiped his mouth, chewing his food before swallowing. "Amazing food, and I appreciate the dedicated work these officers of the law do, protecting people, keeping peace. It brings me joy to be in their company and look out for them."

Made sense, since Ares was the god of war and civil order.

I returned to my meal. The tacos tasted divine, the seasoned fish melting on my tongue. I slouched, every muscle relaxed, and finished my first one, then reached for another. "Pretty sure I can eat ten of these bad boys."

"Babe, I'll order you as many as you want." Ares smiled so gently, I beamed, unable to believe how much he'd changed since I first met him.

"We should definitely go for gelato after this," Apollo added.

"Nobody wants gelato." Ares chuckled. "It's a girl's desert."

"That's bull." Apollo stiffened.

"Have to agree with Ares on this one," Poseidon pipped in.

"I'll go with you," I said to Apollo. "I like gelato."

"See," Ares said a bit too loudly, drawing others attention. "Point proven."

And all of them burst into laughter. I snuggled against Apollo and leaned in for a kiss. "I expect ice cream after this meal, you know that?"

"Anything for you, sweetheart."

We sat there, eating, laughing, discussing the true origin of gelato, and I couldn't have been happier. Sometimes the simplest things were the best. I had three gods in my life who cared for me, adored me, and wanted nothing more than to make me smile. This was the kind of life I'd yearned for, although I couldn't help it as my mind sailed to Hades. What exactly was he doing now?

CHAPTER 25

Apollo

I waited for Elyse in front of her apartment. I'd stopped at the florist and bought her roses. Red ones, the color of blood, the color of love.

We'd agreed to meet tonight as she'd been with Poseidon most of the day, and I missed her. I wanted to spend as much time with her as possible. The past week, since we'd fought X in the Underworld, each of us had been with her, splitting up the time between us. The others kept an eye on her friend, Catina in case X returned. Elyse trained harder, and the three of us had scoured Chicago to see if X would pop his oily head out at any point.

He hadn't shown himself, but neither had Hades.

I had no idea where the two of them were. I hoped that they weren't together, in cahoots somehow. But since Hades had arrived to help us fight X, I was starting to think the guy didn't want this world to have a bad ending after all. Maybe he was working on holding X in the Underworld to prevent any more damage on Earth, but it wasn't like he shared anything with us.

Who would have known Hades could be a hero? I didn't know why or how he'd changed his mind about being on our side, but he had, and that was what mattered.

I glanced at the screen of my phone, looking at the time. Elyse should have come home around six with Poseidon, but tonight she was taking longer. I didn't panic, or think something had happened to her. She'd lost all of her extra lives, and she was down to the last one before her death was final, but she'd changed. She'd become a lot more responsible, and she looked after herself.

Having spare lives to keep you safe was a burden as much as a blessing. We'd all noticed that Elyse behaved differently, showing us that maybe she hadn't taken her regenerating as seriously as she should have. And as long as she didn't die one more time, everything was going to be okay.

The atmosphere shifted, the air growing thicker, and I stared into the sky. I wasn't sure what I was feeling. At first, I thought it might be X searching for Elyse at her apartment. But what surrounded me wasn't darkness.

They were storm clouds. Poseidon?

A moment later, the heavens opened up and Zeus descended from the sky, carrying lightning bolts in his hands, thunder rumbling in his wake.

My stomach turned. I hadn't seen him since he made me promise not to fall for a mortal woman again.

"Yo, Zeus, what's up?" I said casually. I tossed the roses behind a trash can.

"You're very chipper for someone who's been fucking with me," Zeus growled. And still thunder rumbled above and lightning flashed around us.

My mind whirled with panic. "I have no idea what you're talking about." I was starting to doubt myself. Zeus was on to me. He had to be. It'd been a while since I'd lain low, taking care no one discovered I was with Elyse. I'd stopped being so careful when there had been no consequences.

"I told you not to date a mortal woman again," Zeus said. "You want to tell me why you're doing just that?"

"Come on, Dad. I'm not just fucking around. We're fighting X; we were all helping her. It's not like it's just some kind of fling. It's for the greater good and all that." I kept my chin lifted, staring at Zeus, at the way his bushy white eyebrows pulled together in a straight line.

"You can help her save the world without sleeping with her," Zeus pointed out.

Of course, he was right.

"And you were dating her before you began helping

her," he continued, his voice climbing. "Don't try to trick me."

My heart raced. "Just give me one more chance."

He sighed. "I asked you to stay away from her. Never see her again."

I couldn't do that. I couldn't stay away from Elyse. It wasn't just because I'd fallen in love with her. She was part of me now, her power taking up space in my heart. Elyse completed me in ways I'd never felt with anyone before, mortal or divine.

"No," I argued. "I can't do that. Look into my heart, see how I feel about her. See what this is doing for me, for the others, for her. Don't tell me to walk away." I spoke deeply, concealing my dread of losing Elyse.

He looked at me for a long time, his heavenly blue eyes pensive. I knew he was doing what I had asked him.

"I see what she means to you." His tone calmed, and I held on to that hope. "And I see how well this unity is working to defeat X."

Something in me relaxed, and I let out a breath.

"But you and I had a deal," he said, shaking his head. "And you broke it."

He lifted his hand and the clouds churned. Lightning started jumping back and forth between his hands like static, thunder clapped loudly, and I cried out.

"Zeus, no!" Dread crawled into my head, numbing me.

In a booming voice, Zeus pronounced, "I hereby

ban you to Mount Olympus, never able to visit Earth again."

A loud clap of thunder drowned out everything else, and I was struck by lightning. I had the sensation of falling, and I screamed, trying to fight this curse. But no matter what I did, his power was stronger than anything I'd ever have, and I shot through the sky back to Mount Olympus.

I crashed into my palace, falling onto the marble floor in the entrance hall. I'd never been this unhappy to be home. I jumped up and ran to the doors then crossed the green grass, trying to get to the gate that would allow me out and back to Earth, back to Elyse.

But the gates were locked. I grabbed the gold bars with both hands and pulled and yanked with all my might, but I couldn't open them.

I let out a cry that sounded like my own version of thunder. Mount Olympus was to be my prison from now on, forevermore. And I'd never see Elyse again. It had all happened so quickly while I'd let down my guard. Waves of grief washed over me, and my body convulsed with each strike. All I remembered was the brightness of her mocha eyes, the details of her face, and now despair pressed in my mind.

She wouldn't know where I'd gone, why I'd disappeared. All she'd know was I'd abandoned her without a reason until one of the other gods found out where I was and told her. But I'd never be able to hold her again, touch her again, kiss her again. I wouldn't be able to fight for her again.

I hadn't even been able to say goodbye.

***

Ready to jump into Hades Is Mine? He was fallen… but to Elyse, Hades would always be a hero. Even if he didn't see it himself.

ABOUT MILA YOUNG

Mila Young tackles everything with the zeal and bravado of the fairytale heroes she grew up reading about. She slays monsters, real and imaginary, like there's no tomorrow. By day she rocks a keyboard as a marketing extraordinaire. At night she battles with her might pen-sword, creating fairytale retellings, and sexy ever after tales. In her spare time, she loves pretending she's a mighty warrior, walks on the beach with her dogs, cuddling up with her cats, and devouring every fantasy tale she can get her pinkies on.

Ready to read more from Mila Young? Subscribe to her newsletter for latest updates and new releases:
www.subscribepage.com/milayoung

For more information...
milayoungauthor@gmail.com

61448888R00172

Made in the USA
Middletown, DE
19 August 2019